I dedicate this novel to my wife, Prunella, and my family who have put up with me all through my life. It is also dedicated to all the people of Cyprus, who delighted me with their hospitality, generosity and wonderful stories during the many years I lived on that wonderful island. My family and I have for a long time considered it our second home and I love to see the smiles on the faces of my family whenever we come back home to Cyprus.

The story is based on a true life incident that happened in the early nineteen eighties and I personally have scuba dived on every dive described in the book and have seen and felt every detail recalled in the story. I only hope that many more scuba divers will enjoy the delights of diving in Cyprus and help to conserve the wonderful that is Cyprus underwater.

All rights reserved

© Copyright Protected

Chapel Cave

Clive Sanders

Chapter 1
Friday, 7th August 1987

Splash!

Peter dropped into the clear warm water of the Mediterranean Sea at the foot of the cave, known to local scuba divers as Chapel Cave, which lay beneath the church of Ayioi Anargiroi, near Cape Greco in Cyprus. He quickly blew out the small amount of water from the bottom of his face mask, checked that all his scuba diving equipment was working fine. Then he turned and looked to the two other divers who were also checking out their gear, before they dropped down on their first dives at this picturesque location.

When Peter was satisfied that they were all ready to commence their dive, he looked back at the ledge below the cave, where they had just stepped off and nodded to his little Cyprus poodle friend, Franz. His little friend was already anxiously pawing at the water with his front foot, knowing that his master was just about to disappear underwater again. Franz was a lovely fluffy Cyprus poodle who reminded Peter of the late Emperor Franz Joseph of Austria, hence his name. Franzie was very popular with the visiting divers, so Peter always insisted on bringing him along on all the dives he ran, as he viewed it as a clear selling advantage against other diving companies in the area.

After Franzie had given his final worried yelp, Peter gave the 'Dive' signal to his two visiting divers and they all let out the air in their buoyancy aids. This enabled them to drop beneath the surface of the sea on to the rocky ledges a few feet below them. The rocks had many sunken pockets in them, which appeared to have been created by a porous sub-strata, dropping down beneath the harder top layer of black stone. Soon the rocks led them down to the sandy sea bed and the divers were surrounded by shoals of beautifully coloured small fish, which fascinated Peter's visiting divers.

+ + + + +

Life had not always been kind to Peter. He had originally been found abandoned as a baby in a public park in Sheffield, an industrial city in the North of England. The children's home he had grown up in had given him the name Peter Parks, due to the location of his discovery. The children's home was been run by the Roman Catholic Church, so Peter had witnessed and experienced a lot of abuse, this helped him to forge a strong resistance in himself. Thus by the age of 12 years, Peter could defend himself very well against most predators and had little to fear from the other children in the home. He left the home at 15 years of age and after 3 years of drifting around on the edge of the criminal element in Sheffield, he joined the British Army at the age of 18 years.

He originally wanted to become an Infantry soldier, but due to his colour perception status, he had been advised to enlist in the Royal Corps of Signals. So in early 1964 he began his Basic

Infantry Training at Catterick Camp in Yorkshire. He instantly liked the discipline and order of being a soldier and found pride in being able to complete all aspects of his training with ease. This resulted in him becoming Best Recruit of his troop.

On the completion of his Basic Infantry Training, Peter was sent to a Royal Signals Training Squadron at Garats Hay in Leicestershire. There he was to learn how to become an Intercept Operator, trained to intercept the Morse communications of potential enemy armies. Peter found the Morse training very challenging, but he eventually passed the course and was subsequently posted to a Royal Signals regiment in West Germany. His new regiment was tasked with intercepting Russian Army communications with the aim of providing warning of a potential Russian attack on West Germany.

During his time in Germany, Peter formed a strong friendship with another young soldier, who lived in York. This friend had a pretty young sister called Carol, who Peter eventually met and fell in love with. Peter and Carol were married in 1967 and in November of that year, they took over a flat near Peter's camp and set up home together. But Carol soon grew disillusioned with the life of an Army wife in Germany and in 1972 they were divorced.

In the meantime, the Army had discovered that Peter possessed a bit of a flair for languages and trained him as a Russian Linguist. When Cyprus was invaded by Turkey in 1974, Peter was given the opportunity of learning Greek, which was followed by a posting to an Army base in Eastern Cyprus in 1975.

Peter quickly fell in love with Cyprus and soon after arriving, Peter joined the Army's scuba diving club in Dhekelia. He also met a beautiful young Cypriot lady, called Elena, who lived in the village near to his Army base. After much courting of both Elena and her family, Peter married Elena in 1977 and for the first time in his life Peter learned the joys of a strong married life with his new Greek family. Peter was honest enough to admit that Elena was really the brains of the business, for she followed her mother's example by taking on the management of the business and the running of their finances.

Elena was been born in Cyprus in the spring of 1951, but moved with her family to London when she was four years of age. Therefore, she always considered herself to be a Greek Cypriot, who had been lucky enough to have a British upbringing and education. Her family moved back to their home village of Vrysoules in eastern Cyprus in 1973. Due to the occupation of Northern Cyprus, property prices in southern Cyprus increased greatly in the years after the invasion and Elena's father saw an opportunity for investment in a plot of land between the village of Ayia Napa and its small fishing harbour. Later, he built a bar and restaurant on the plot of land and as others invested and built in the area, his establishment was soon making a good profit. Peter and Elena rejoiced in her father's success and greatly enjoyed helping to run the bar. Due to Peter's love of the Greek language and culture, he eventually began to take an interest in the Greek Orthodox Church and enjoyed the informality of the services in the local Greek Orthodox Church. Soon afterwards he changed his religious status with the Army to Greek Orthodox.

Elena gladly helped him with his Greek lessons, so that by the time of their wedding his Greek was good enough for him was to play his full part in the service and for him to become fully engaged in conversations with Elena's parents. As time went by, Elena and Peter adopted the practice of speaking Greek when in the company of only Greek speakers, but using English when in the company of English speakers. This they felt was the best way to progress their business efforts and their Greek social circle.

Things appeared to be going well for Peter and Elena, until the Argentine Army invaded the Falkland Islands on 2nd April 1982. Peter was immediately informed that he would be flown back to England to be part of the force being sent south to retake the islands from the Argentines. He was given a set of 'Teach Yourself Spanish' books and audio tapes and on the voyage down to the Falkland Islands he occupied his time by learning Spanish.

Peter never told Elena too much about what he did during the liberation of the Falkland Islands, but she thought that he had been involved in some of the fighting, which resulted in the capitulation of the Argentine Forces on 14th June 1982. Elena did note that when Peter got back to her, for the first time he began to talk over his plans for when he finished his Army career, which focused on starting a scuba diving school alongside her father's bar in Ayia Napa.

Thus, when Peter's Army career finished in 1986, after 22 years serving the colours, he used his end of service financial package to purchase enough scuba gear to establish his diving school in the accommodation Elena's father provided alongside his bar in Ayia Napa. They named their business as the Poseidon Dive Centre, after the ancient Greek god of the sea. Peter had thrown his heart and soul into the diving school and with much support from Elena and her father he was already gaining a good reputation. At forty-one years of age Peter still looked a very fit man, who could easily develop a good relationship with any potential customer, even though most people did spot that there was a hardness in his character, which probably dated back to his bad experiences in his youth.

Shortly after reaching the sandy sea bed, Peter signalled to his visiting divers that they should turn left and head out over a patch of eel grass that was waving backwards and forwards in the currents. Soon they all picked out the shape of a large anchor standing out from the sea bed with the broken remains of countless amphorae surrounding the anchor. Peter indicated for his two divers to pose alongside the anchor and took a few photographs of them with his Nikonos 4 underwater camera. After checking on how much air each of his divers had remaining in the cylinders, he indicated to each of them that they should start working their way back to the exit point at Chapel Cave.

Peter allowed each of his divers to investigate anything that interested them on their way back to their exit point, after a total of just over 20 minutes underwater, their heads broke out of the water very near to the flat rocks of Chapel Cave, much to the delight of Franz the Cyprus poodle, who jumped up and down in joy and barked his approval at their return from the depths.

Peter helped his divers out of the sea, sorted out their equipment for the short climb back to his flatbed truck which was parked in the small car park between the church of Ayioi Anargiroi, after which he gave them a short debrief on all that he had noted on the dive.

He finally helped them out of their diving gear, which was all secured safely in the back of the truck along with Franzie and they began the short drive back to his diving school at Ayia Napa harbour.

Chapter 2
Monday, 10th August 1987

Peter's day routinely started with him pretending not to notice that Elena had woken up, climbed quietly out of bed and tip-toeing down the cool stone stairs to the kitchen where she made him a strong cup of coffee. Peter normally rolled over in the bed when Elena quietly came back into the bedroom, carrying the two cups of coffee she had made and after giving him a soft kiss on his forehead, she announced the time shown on their alarm clock and informed him that it was time to get up.

Franz stirred from his dog basket as Elena placed Peter's coffee mug on his bedside table and with a determined bound, Franz jumped up on the bed to have his ears ruffled by his two favourite people, until eventually he jumped down and sat by Elena's side of the bed, wagging his tail until Peter agreed to take him back down to the kitchen and fill up his bowl with his breakfast of dog meat and biscuits.

The reason Peter loved Franz so much was that shortly after they were married they had found their lovely Cyprus poodle at the British Forces Animal Welfare Service kennels in the Dhekelia Garrison. He had been found abandoned, which Peter very much associated with, so he was very keen to offer this lonely dog a new life.

Once they had showered and eaten a bite of breakfast, Peter drove them all down to their diving centre and Elena, having checked through the centre's booking diary, announced that they only had one booking that morning, which was for a Lebanese diver called Michael Abood. She didn't know too much about this customer, due to his relatively poor standard of English and the lousy quality of the telephone connection between Ayia Napa and wherever he was calling from in Cyprus. All she knew was that he was due to arrive at eleven o'clock and wanted a nice gentle shore dive to familiarize himself with Cyprus diving.

Peter stood in the dive centre's kitchen as he took on board the booking and in his mind started to work out which of the many shore dives he knew in the area would be the most suitable for this diver of unknown background and what gear would be best for the visitor. Without any conscious thoughts he lifted down the two coffee mugs he and Elena most commonly used, opened their coffee jar and added a spoonful of coffee to both mugs. He clicked on the electric kettle and waited for it to boil. Once the kettle had boiled, Peter poured the water into their mugs, added the necessary amount of milk to their coffees and joined Elena in the front office of the dive centre. Franz had already flopped himself down on his favourite blanket and concentrated on guarding his humans from any intruders who might unexpectedly enter the dive centre.

"Did you take the booking from the Lebanese diver?" Peter asked Elena. Elena nodded and said, "His English doesn't seem to be too good, so I really can't tell you any more than that he should be here by eleven o'clock."

Peter nodded and after a short while said, "I think I will take him to Green Bay. As the bay is nice and shallow I can quickly figure out if he will be safe in the water and take him out of the bay and see how he is in a bit deeper water. If he's okay at ten metres, I can take him to Tunnels or Chapel Cave on his next dive."

+ + + + +

The scheduled time for the arrival of the Lebanese diver came and passed with no sign of the expected visiting diver. This was not an uncommon event and Peter merely tapped his watch to show Elena the time and shrugged and went to the working area at the back of the dive centre and began to check the face masks neatly housed on the shelves above the ranged wet suits. He was checking the facemasks to see if there were any with their water seals showing signs of wear or distress. Shortly after 11:20am, a dusty red Nissan Sunny with Cypriot Hire Car number plates pulled up just infront of the dive centre.

Elena, who was still sitting behind her desk in the front office of the dive centre, noticed Franz's head coming up from the blanket and called to Peter that she thought the visiting diver had just turned up.

Peter emerged from the working area just as a dark complexioned man, roughly five feet nine inches entered the dive centre and introduced himself as Michael. Peter estimated his age as just over twenty-five years and noted that although he was quite a slim man and should fit nicely into the red and black wet suit on hook number four.

Michael apologized from being late, but excused himself by saying that he had got a bit lost in the village of Ayia Napa and couldn't see any signposts for the harbour. Then it simply dawned on him to follow the road down from the village, as most harbours are normally at the lowest part of the town.

Peter gladly accepted Michael's excuse and asked him if he would like a cup of coffee. Michael certainly had no problem understanding the question and asked whether the coffee was Instant coffee or was it Turkish coffee? Peter smiled at the question and simply stated that he only had Nescafe Instant coffee and Michael accepted the offer with only a small look of disappointment noticeable on his face.

When Peter brought the coffees out from the kitchen he found Michael and Elena sitting in the two comfortable chairs in the front office, with Michael obviously enjoying the conversation with such a good looking, young Cypriot lady. Peter placed Michael's coffee on the table between the two chairs and put his coffee on the desk top and leant on the desk while he let Michael and Elena carry on chatting about the dangers of driving on Cypriot roads.

Eventually, after Michael assured Elena that Lebanese roads were safer than Cypriot ones, Peter managed to enter the conversation by stating that he believed Michael wanted to have a few easy shore dives with him. Michael, nodded and said in good English, but spoken in a slightly higher tone than was normal in most people and with an odd pronunciation of the letter 'h', that he had learned to dive with a dive centre just outside Beirut, near where he had grown up. His parents ran a successful clothing store in Beirut, but due to the on-going Civil War in the country, his family had moved out of the Lebanon and were now renting accommodation in Larnaca until the situation in Beirut got back to normal.

Michael had qualified as an Open Water Diver with the local dive centre, which adopted the standards of the American Professional Association of Diving Instructors (PADI) organization, but he seemed somewhat guarded when Peter asked to see his qualifications, so Peter pragmatically accepted that Michael could be a qualified PADI diver, but he could easily check this out when he took Michael for his first shore dive in Green Bay.

At this point Peter brought up the subject of payment and advised Michael that the normal charge for an Open Water Check-out Dive was thirty Cypriot pounds and was just about to offer Michael a discount, when Michael pulled out his wallet and instantly paid out the required amount with no hesitation, so Peter dismissed in his mind the idea of a discount.

Elena next asked Michael to fill out the usual forms that were always required from visiting divers. These basically consisted of a general medical form, plus details of diving qualifications and contact details in case of a mishap.

Michael queried one of two of the questions, but eventually the forms were completed to Elena's satisfaction and after a quick run through the normal safety lectures, Peter briefed Michael on his proposed schedule of dives. He explained that he planned to take Michael on a very easy 'check-out' dive at a place called Green Bay and if all went well on the dive, their next dive would be a bit more adventurous and interesting.

Michael stated that he was happy with this plan, so Peter took him into the working area at the back of the dive centre, picked out the wet suit that hung on hook number four, which did indeed fit Michael like a glove and once Michael had pulled on the wet suit boots Peter handed to him, the two of them climbed into Peter's flatbed truck that we already loaded with all the diving equipment they would need for the dive. Franz jumped up on to the truck and moved to his normal place, sitting in the back of the truck with his head facing towards the tailgate, they headed back towards the centre of Ayia Napa and on to the road to Cape Greco, which would eventually take them to Green Bay.

+ + + + +

During the drive to Green Bay, Michael appeared quite happy to chat to Peter about the diving he had done in the Lebanon and also about the troubles that the country was going through in its internal Civil War and the recent invasion of the southern part of the country by Israel.

Michael informed Peter that his family had its roots in the mountainous north of Lebanon. It was thought that his family had originally been farmers, but at some point in the family history, some of his male ancestors grew to become important members of the ancient Maronite Christian faith, which led to the family moving nearer the capital of Lebanon in Beirut.

Michael considered himself to be a lapsed member of the Maronite community and always thought of himself as more cosmopolitan than most of his countrymen. He greatly admired American Hollywood action movies, which had spurred him into learning how to scuba dive. Peter noted that not once in their conversation had Michael asked how much he would be asked to pay for his dives, which Peter took as a sign that Michael's family were fairly well-off and he didn't have to worry too much about money.

Eventually, Peter turned off the Tarmacked road and drove the truck down a sandy track, with large boulders encroaching on either side, until they came to a small headland, with a scenic bay on the left-hand side of the small cape.

Franzie was instantly bouncing around the back of the truck as Peter and Michael climbed out of the cab and Peter opened up the tailgate. Peter then briefed Michael on the details of the dive, before he began to load up Michael with his diving equipment.

Once Michael was fully kitted out, Peter put on his own diving gear and led Michael down over the rocks to the small sandy entrance to the bay. Warning Michael of the rocky outcrops on the floor of the bay, Peter held Michael's arm and gently guided him out into the bay until the water came up to the top of their chests.

Peter showed Michael how to spit into his facemask and spread the saliva over the inside of the lenses, then having made sure that Michael had fitted his mask on correctly, he showed Michael how the Diving Regulator worked and when everything seemed to be working well, Peter gave the signal to 'Dive' and they both settled down on their knees with the sea water just over their heads.

Peter ran through several basic drills with Michael and noted that he clearly had done quite a few dives previously and seemed perfectly happy with all that was going on. So Peter indicated to Michael that they should go deeper and they headed off to the mouth of the bay.

As they left the bay, they finned over a collection of large rocks, which hosted a large number of small fish. Then they the dropped down to the sandy sea bed, which lay before them.

Peter became more and more convinced that Michael had clearly done quite a lot of diving and so was glad to let Michael take the lead and only when the pressure gauges on the cylinders indicated that they were nearing the safety level of 50 bar, did Peter indicate to Michael that he should follow Peter back to their exit point in the bay.

As they stood up in the waist deep water and removed their fins, Peter slapped Michael on the back and congratulated him on the way he had handled himself during the dive. Michael responded well to the praise and by the time they had de-kitted themselves and dried off the majority of the water, they were already showing signs that a good friendship was already in the making.

Peter quickly packed all the diving gear and Franz safely settled in the back of the truck and they drove back the eight miles to the dive centre in good time. After a final debrief Peter suggested that if Michael had the time, they could grab a quick lunch and a drink in the bar owned by Elena's father.

Over lunch Elena asked how the dive had gone and Peter happily reported that all had gone well and turning to Michael he asked if he would like to do another dive. Michael wiped some mayonnaise from the corner of his mouth as he swallowed another mouthful of his Halloumi and Chips lunch and nodded as he tried to say that he would love to go on another dive. So before Michael drove off back to Larnaca, it was agreed that he would come back the next day for another dive, which would be a bit more challenging than the first.

+ + + + +

That evening Peter and Elena drove to the village of Xylotymbou, which was situated in the British controlled

Eastern Sovereign Base Area (ESBA) of Cyprus, less than a mile from the major British Garrison town of Dhekelia. In the centre of the village lay the home of a carpenter named, Taki Papakyriakou, who was a distant cousin of Elena's father. This carpenter had provided all the wood work in their home when they were married and over the years had become a very good friend to both of them. They often visited his house where Peter would present Taki with a bottle of his favourite Scotch whisky, Johnnie Walker Black Label, which Peter could easily obtain duty-free from old British Army friends. They would then would sit in Taki's front room, drinking Cypriot Anglias brandy and chatting about life in Cyprus. Taki delighted in educating Peter about the history of Cyprus and the Greek Orthodox faith.

On a previous occasion Taki had enthralled Peter with the story of the infamous Locust Egg Tax, which was imposed on the population of Cyprus by the last Turkish ruler of Cyprus and was then continued by the British authorities after they took over the island in the 1860s. He continued that under the rules of the Locust Egg Tax every year each man on the island was compelled to collect 8 okes, roughly 20 kilograms in weight, of locust eggs and hand them in to the authorities. He added that the castle at Paphos Harbour was one of the places where the eggs had to be handed in to. Naturally, richer men did not want to go out and collect all that weight of locust eggs, so the Turks, being very shrewd business men, allowed rich men to buy the eggs from them and hand them back in. Eventually, there were no more locust eggs on the island and the tax became just a paper exercise, where you paid the tax and got a piece of paper that said you had collected 8 okes of eggs.

Peter always enjoyed these evenings, although Elena often grew bored with Taki endless lectures and would often stray out to the family kitchen and chat with Taki's wife, Maria, about the hardships of a married woman's life in Cyprus.

That evening was no exception, for after exchanging pleasantries on their arrival, they settled down on the comfortable chairs in Taki's front room and Maria went into the kitchen to make coffees for everyone. Maria liked the local Nescafe instant coffee, which had a much stronger flavour than the Nescafe found in northern Europe. Taki asked about the health of Elena's father and mother and followed this on with his usual enquiry about how soon it would be before they had their first child, which was always Elena's excuse to go and join Maria in the kitchen. Peter was left to explain that they wanted to wait for their first child until their finances were in a more stable condition, to which Taki gave his customary snort and extolled Peter that it was the duty of every married man to have a son as soon as possible. So that he could pass on the family business to him, while he still had time to enjoy his life.

Luckily Maria came back with the coffees at the best moment to interrupt her husband, before he began his detailed advice on the best ways to make babies. As they sipped their coffees, Peter asked about how Taki's children were progressing, which he knew was very safe ground as Taki was very proud indeed of how well his two sons, Haralambos and Alexandros, and his lovely daughter, Cressida, were doing in their lives. Haralambos had studied music in Athens and was a very popular concert pianist in Greece. Alexandros was gradually taking over the carpentry business from his father, but Taki always pointed out that he was still making mistakes and it would be some years before he finally handed over the business to him. Then, to complete his family briefing, Taki added that Cressida had married a doctor who practiced in Limassol and was expecting her first child, which Taki was sure would be a healthy son.

When the coffees had been drunk, Taki pulled out a packet of Benson and Hedges cigarettes, which clearly bore the NAAFI (Navy, Army and Air Force Institutes) markings that showed that he somehow had got hold of another packet of duty free cigarettes. He offered the cigarettes to Peter, knowing well that Peter did not smoke, before he had lit his own cigarette and settled deep into his chair, put his feet up on a small stool and resumed his history of the Greek Orthodox Church. This started with a gentle revision of his last lesson with the question, "So Peter, do you remember who founded the Christian Church in Cyprus?"

Peter replied, "Yes, it was the Apostle Barnabas."

"Excellent." Said Taki, "He arrived in Cyprus with Saint Paul and Mark the Evangelist in the year forty-five. They landed in Salamis and travelled all over Cyprus preaching the Christian faith until the finally reached Paphos, where they left to spread the faith in other countries. Later, in the year fifty, Barnabas and Mark returned to Cyprus and founded the first Christian Church at Salamis, which today is just outside Famagusta. Did you know that Saint Barnabas is the Patron Saint of Cyprus?"

When Peter nodded, for Taki has told him loud and long all about Saint Barnabas only last week, Taki continued, "We could not have a better Patron Saint than our blessed Saint Barnabas. He performed many miracles in his time in Cyprus. He was even born in Cyprus, but no one knows where. His miracles include healing many sick people in Salamis, Amathus and Kition and he also sent back a plague of locusts that had come from Egypt. But he is remembered most for the fact that he rid the island of Cyprus from snakes."

Peter thought this fact through for a minute or two, for he was sure he had heard a very similar story about Saint Patrick in Ireland, so he finally said, "Then how come you still have so many snakes in Cyprus?"

Taki stared as him for just a moment and replied, "Only because the Turks brought them back again."

Chapter 3
Tuesday, 11th August 1987

Michael was already waiting infront of the dive centre as Elena and Peter, with Franzie in his usual place in the back of the truck, arrived the next morning. Michael had been smoking when they drove up, so as he started to walk towards them, he threw his partly smoked cigarette to the ground and stepped on it as he approached them.

After shaking hands with Peter and Elena, Michael explained that his father had given him a lift to the dive centre as he wanted to explore the village that was believed to be on the way to becoming a major tourist attraction for the south-east corner of the island. He added that his father would be picking him up from the dive centre in the early afternoon, so if Peter could take him for another shore dive that morning, he would be very pleased.

This fitted in well with Peter's plan, which was to take Michael on another not-too-deep dive at a dive site known as Tunnels. Peter explained that Tunnels was very near the headland of Cape Greco and featured an underwater tunnel that was quite spectacular. Michael stated that this sounded ideal, as long as they got back to the dive centre by early afternoon.

So as Elena opened up the dive centre, Peter sorted out the equipment he and Michael would need for the dive and in very short order, Peter and Michael climbed into the cab of their flatbed truck and after a final wave to Elena, they set off for the drive to Tunnels, with Franzie sitting comfortably on top of the diving equipment.

The drive to Tunnels took them initially up through the village of Ayia Napa and after that, they turned right and headed towards Cape Greco. The narrow road climbed steadily as they drove higher towards the large mass of Cape Greco. Soon they began to see the large Radar dish that was situated on the highest point of Cape Greco and had its very large dish pointing nearly horizontally in a north-easterly direction. This dish was located in a small British Military compound and local rumour was that it was part of an early warning Radar chain with the aim of identifying the early launch of a Russian missile attack against the Western Powers.

As they approached the Radar dish, the road split into two with one road heading north towards Fig Tree Bay and Protaras, with the other road heading south-east towards the tip of the Cape Greco peninsular. Peter took the road that dropped down towards the Cape Greco headland.

The road was very narrow and Peter ignored the turn off that led to the Radar site, but carefully followed the road downhill towards the headland of the Cape, which had been sealed off with a strong well-maintained steel fence. Inside the fence were a small number of buildings and several tall Radio masts, which was the home of a radio station called 'Radio Free Europe'. This radio station was funded by the United States government and broadcast western pop music and news to the nations surrounding Cyprus. Once again there was local gossip that the radio station was part of a CIA operation and transmitted messages to CIA agents all around the Middle East.

As they drove down a particularly steep stretch of the narrow road, they could clearly see the radio station ahead of them, but about two hundred yards or so before the gates of the radio station, there was a turn-off to the right, which led down a well-used track to a patch of ground that clearly served as a car park. In fact there was already a black flatbed truck parked up in this area, with a small party of four divers getting kitted up for a dive.

Peter recognized the vehicle and told Michael, that one of his close diving buddies and competing diving instructor, Ian Murray, had got to the dive site even earlier than they had. He assured Michael that he would like Ian, who was a Scouser from Liverpool and was always great fun to be around.

Peter soon parked their flatbed truck, close to the other and getting out of the cab, he walked across to the other diving party and slapped the smallest member of the party on the back, saying, "You must have got up really early today, Ian. I thought we would have the place to ourselves at this time of the morning."

Ian smiled at Peter and replied, "Good morning to you too, Pete. You know what they say, the early diver always gets the visibility."

Ian next introduced his divers, all of whom were members of the British Sub-Aqua Club (BSAC), who had flown out together from Coventry, in the UK for a short diving holiday and had booked a series of dives with Ian during their stay.

Peter, in turn, introduced Michael to them and told them the basic details about Michael's diving career. Michael did not really seem to like the idea of diving with another group of divers, but Peter explained that Ian was a real expert on this dive and he was sure that Michael would enjoy the dive even more due to Ian's extensive knowledge of the dive site.

Peter helped Michael to put on all his diving equipment, as Ian played with Franz, who was obviously happy in his company, as he explained to the combined dive party about the dive they were about to enjoy.

As part of his brief, Ian pointed to a hole in the rock, through which sea water occasionally lapped out of the hole. He explained that this hole led into an underwater cave, which if they elected to, he would show them how to exit through the hole at the end of the dive, but he considered it a bit too risky for the party to start the dive by going into the sea through the hole.

He pointed to where the flat rocks on which they were standing, met the sea and informed them that the safest way to enter the sea on this dive was simply by stepping off the ledge, at the end of the cave and dropping into the sea, which was about ten feet deep at this point.

Ian continued his brief by explaining that the sea stayed at about ten feet deep for some distance and soon started to drop away before them. When they reached this drop-off, they would turn right and start to head south-west to where they would find the tunnel that the dive was named after. He added that in the tunnel there were a few examples of lace coral growing, which he strongly advised the divers to leave untouched, as lace coral was pretty rare around Cyprus and in the name of conservation, he requested them to treat it with all their respect. He added that it took many years for lace coral to grow a few inches, so to be careful not to rub against it during the dive.

Ian stopped for a moment to emphasize the point about the lace coral, then he continued by saying that if they looked carefully at the sides and roof of the tunnel they would see marks that some people insisted showed that the tunnel had been hand-carved at some time in its history, but no one could explain how this was done when the tunnel was so deep underwater.

He also stated that when they had seen enough of the tunnel, he would lead them further eastwards and show them some interesting ancient Greek graves, which were now some twenty metres underwater and once again no one he knew how to explain how these ancient graves were to be found in such deep water.

By the time Ian had finished his briefing, Peter and Michael were fully kitted up and ready to go, so Ian led the way to the edge of the water and after checking that all his divers were ready to enter the water, he gave an 'OK' signal and stepped off the ledge and into the sea.

He quickly floated back up to the surface and checked his equipment. Then he turned and signalled to one of his divers to join him in the water. Soon all the visiting divers, including Michael had entered the sea and Peter joined them as tail-end Charlie or last diver in.

Ian, once again, exchanged 'OK' signals with all the divers and gestured to them to vent their Buoyancy Aids of air, so that they could drop down under water. Once Ian was happy that everyone was okay, he turned and headed out away from the shore, over a sea-bed that consisted of sandy-covered rocks. When he reached the point where the rocks started to drop away ahead of him, he turned right and led the party for another few hundred yards, before he stopped and pointed at the opening of a tunnel, which was about six feet in height, ten feet in width and stretched back up the slope for about fifty feet. The tunnel was pretty thought-provoking, as it really looked as though it was man-made. The curvature of the ceiling of the tunnel simply looked too regular to be natural rock and Peter watched as Michael and one of Ian's divers ran their hands over the smooth-ish rock and shook their heads at each other in surprise at the unnatural features of the tunnel.

A few minutes later, Ian hand-signalled to them to look at what he was showing them and all the divers realized that he was pointing at a small piece of lace coral. Having checked that all the divers were looking in his direction, he signalled that they should be careful near it and not to touch it.

When the divers emerged from the shallow end of the tunnel, Ian held up the pressure gauge of his cylinder and checked that each of the divers had enough air left to progress on to the next part of the dive. When he was satisfied that everyone had sufficient air left in their tanks, he signalled for them to follow him westwards and down the slope ahead of them.

After another two hundred yards, Ian turned and looking at the other divers, indicated that they should check out a sunken area in the nearby rocks and the visiting divers gradually realized that the sunken areas were somewhat rectangular in shape and had flattish bottoms. This prompted them to remember Ian's briefing, when he talked about ancient Greek graves and one after each other the visiting divers nodded sagely to Ian, indicating that they now realized what they were looking at.

At this point of the dive, Peter swam up to Ian and indicated to him to look a bit further down the slope. Ian peered in the direction that Peter indicated and after a short time, noticed that there were two apparently new building breeze blocks, tied together on the sea bed, with what looked like a blue nylon rope leading up above them. The breeze blocks had no marine life or crustacean on them at all, which indicated that they had not been in the sea for very long.

Peter indicated to Ian that he should stay where he was with the visiting divers, while Peter investigated this strange sight. When Ian nodded in agreement, Peter finned rapidly down the slope to investigate the breeze blocks. Noting that he was now nearly 30 metres underwater, Peter checked out the breeze blocks, which did indeed look as if they had only been dropped into place in the last few days, he inspected the blue nylon line leading up towards the surface above the breeze blocks. He found that the line appeared to be a very strong fishing line and when he pulled down on the line, he could feel that it was attached to something above them which contained a lot of buoyancy.

As Peter attempted to pull down on the line, he turned and found that Ian was leading down the other divers as Ian joined Peter in his attempts to pull down the source of buoyancy above them.

Suddenly, with no warning at all, Ian pulled out his diving knife and cut through the blue nylon fishing line. The cut line immediately shot up through the water and rapidly disappeared above them. Peter looked quizzically at Ian, but Ian merely shrugged and pointed back up the slope towards the place where they would exit the dive. Mildly annoyed at Ian's actions, Peter followed the diving party back up the slope until the cave, where they had entered the sea, appeared before them.

Ian stopped in the entrance to the cave and by hand signal, asked each of the divers, including Michael, if they would like to go through the cave and exit via the hole in the rock ceiling, but none of them took up Ian's offer, so Ian and Peter helped the visiting divers to climb out of the sea on to the dry rock roof of the cave.

Once everyone was out of the sea, Peter pulled out his regulator and demanded to know why Ian had cut the fishing line above the breeze blocks. Ian replied by saying, "There was an story in the Cyprus Mail last week about drug smugglers using a very similar method of smuggling in drugs, but tying them to a heavy weight and leaving packages of drugs floating a few metres below the surface of the sea, so that the drug importers simply had to find them, then swim down a few metres to cut the rope to the weights and retrieve the drugs. I can't think of any other reason why someone would do that, besides something illegal like drug smuggling."

Peter had not read the article in the Cyprus Mail, but agreed with Ian's assumption that it did seem a real possibility, so he looked out over the sea in the direction of where they had been diving, but could not see anything out of the ordinary in any direction he looked, so he simply put the subject to the back of his mind, gave Franzie a well-deserved cuddle and helped to Michael to take off his diving kit and get ready for the drive back to the dive centre.

They arrived back at the dive centre shortly after noon and Peter cleaned off their diving gear as Elena chatted to Michael and accepted Michael's payment for the dive. She quickly made all three of them coffees, which Peter managed to drink before it got too cold.

For a little while they chatted about the dive and Michael explained to Elena about the floating object they had found tied up to the breeze blocks and Ian's explanation for what they had discovered.

Elena, ever the business conscious member to the team, she asked Michael if he would like to book up any more dives, but Michael responded by saying that he thought his father had got a few business trips planned for him over the next few days, so if everyone was okay with this situation, he would call them as soon as he had a day clear for some more diving.

Elena and Peter were more than happy with this arrangement, mainly because they had a few bookings coming up during the remainder of the week and although Peter clearly enjoyed taking Michael diving, he did have other customers to consider.

Shortly after 2pm, a fairly shiny Mercedes saloon pulled up near to the diving centre and Michael announced the arrival of his father. Michael's father quickly impressed both Elena and Peter. He was well-dressed for the time of year, wearing a business-like neat white short-sleeved shirt, with tidily pressed light slacks and comfortable looking neat shoes. He looked to be in his mid-fifties and clearly seemed to be a confident, worldly-wise cosmopolitan business man.

Michael introduced his father to Elena and Peter and then explained to his father that he had enjoyed the two dives Peter had already taken him on and hoped that he would be able to do a lot more diving with his new-found diving friend.

Michael's father, cheerfully shook hands with both Elena and Peter and when Elena offered him a cup of coffee, politely explained that he was a little bit peckish. Michael had already explained that Elena's father had a nearby restaurant that offered good food, so why don't they all have a nice relaxed lunch, before he took Michael back home to his mother.

Everyone agreed that a light lunch would be a good idea, especially as there were no bookings for diving that afternoon, so Elena settled Franz down in his dog basket and locked up the dive centre and after a short while, they moved into the bar restaurant next door that was owned and run by Elena's father, George.

George's real name was Yiorgos in Greek, but as he had originally been introduced to Peter as 'George', Peter continued to use the Anglicised version of his name.

As they entered through the door, George looked over from the bar where he had been serving four men, all of whom looked to be in their middle forties and smiled and nodded at Elena and her party. Elena led the way to the table that the family tended to occupy when they used the bar, Elena and Peter sat on one side of the table and Michael and his father sat on the other, with their backs towards the bar.

A few moments later George came over to their table and gave Elena a quick kiss on her cheek before he pulled up another chair and shook hands with everyone at the table. Peter introduced Michael and his father, who informed everyone that his name was Rami. George asked what everyone wanted to drink and after a few minutes of pleasantries, he went back to the bar to serve their drinks.

Peter was sitting with his back to wall and as he chatted at the table, he was subconsciously keeping aware of the other four people in the bar. He noticed that they kept glancing at his table and that from the looks on their faces, they did not appear to be the happiest group of men he had ever seen.

All of the four men were well-built and sun-tanned. They all had dark hair, which on two of the men had flecks of grey sprinkled through their hair. The men were muscular and wearing working clothes that showed many signs of wear. They were drinking from bottles of Cypriot Keo beer, which did not seem to be having too much effect on their dispositions.

By this time, Michael's father, Rami, was telling them about how the family ended up in Cyprus. He explained that his family had lived for many years in the mountainous countryside of North Lebanon. It was believed that the family had been there since even before the Christian Church spread into the Lebanon and there were even stories that their ancestors had been priests to the old religions of Lebanon. Eventually the family became members of the Maronite faith and this had brought them to Beirut, the capital city of Lebanon. Rami's father refused to follow the family tradition of becoming a Maronite official and instead learned to be a tailor and eventually ran a very successful business in Beirut.

As Rami continued to relate the family history, one of the men at the bar stood up and started to walk towards their table, which was noted by Peter and he watched the man from the corner of his eye as he approached their table. As he neared their table, the man took a slight detour and headed towards the door that led to the toilets.

With some relief Peter, turned again to Rami's history of the Abood family, with Rami telling of how the impact of the fighting that was now taking place in Lebanon had resulted in the family deciding to move to the safety of Cyprus for as long as the Civil War lasted in their homeland.

Peter became aware that the man who had gone to the toilet had come back out of the door and was walking casually back to the bar and his three friends. When the man climbed back on to his barstool he indicated for his friends to huddle towards him as he quietly told them something. Whatever he said made the other three men look across to Peter's table with mixed looks of interest and hostility. Peter considered telling the others at his table of what he had noticed, when the tallest of the four man pushed his barstool back from the bar and began to slowly walk towards their table.

When the man reached the table he stood behind Rami's chair and glowered down at each of the people sitting at the table. Gradually the conversation around the table died down until everyone was looking over Rami's shoulder at the man and even Rami stopped telling his family history and quickly glanced over his shoulder at the man behind him.

Peter had seen this sort of behaviour many times before. He had seen it in the Children's home he had grown up in and many times during his years in the Army. It was the behaviour of a bully who was used to getting his own way by instilling fear in others. Peter knew there was only one possible outcome of the situation and that was by acting very quickly and causing the bully such pain that he would back away from the fight. Peter slowly moved his feet into the position that would allow him to stand up very quickly in a firm stance, so that he could land a heavy punch to the centre to the bully's face, which would hopefully disable him quickly.

The man standing behind Rami's chair coughed, and in a voice that was heavily laden with threat said, "So, you are from the Lebanon, that nation of cowards and suicide bombers."

When there was no reaction from those sitting around the table, the man slapped Rami on the side of his head and started to speak again, but before he could start his first word, Peter shot to his feet and landed a heavy punch on to the nose of the bully. In shock, the bully stumbled backwards and fell over a chair behind him, which brought the other three men to their feet.

Peter shouted to those around the table to get out of the bar as quickly as possible as he pushed aside the table and with his head down rushed towards the bully. He knew that he had very little time indeed to deliver a devastating blow to the bully, before his reinforcements arrived at the table. The bully was pulling himself to his feet when Peter managed to kick him as hard as he could in the face. The bully's head shot back and

Peter began to believe that his strategy had been correct, but he suddenly felt his left arm being pulled violently back, so he swung around as fast as he could and aimed a blow at his new assailant. The sudden surge of adrenaline that was sweeping through his body seemed to slow down everything that was happening, so as Peter's fist moved towards the face of the new attacker, he saw that the man's left hand had successfully blocked the punch and before he could start to throw a new punch, the new attacker reacted with such speed that all Peter could do was try to duck the punch that was rapidly moving towards his face.

Peter felt the impact of the heavy punch on his cheekbone and as he tried to blindly strike back at his foe, another very heavy punch hit him on his right jaw and Peter was aware that he was now surrounded by all four men. Peter was a very strong believer in only fighting battles that you stood a chance of winning, so quickly decided that this was one fight he could never win and dropped down on the floor in a foetal position with his hands hugging his head for protection.

The next thing he felt was a strong kick to his abdomen, followed by a barrage of kicks to his head and back, until unconsciousness came to his aid and he passed out.

Chapter 4
Wednesday, 12th August 1987

Peter suddenly came to in a strange bed. His eyes opened and he saw a white ceiling above him as he carefully looked around himself, then he saw he was in hospital ward with Elena sitting by the side of his bed holding his hand.

Elena stood up and thanking the Lord that he had finally come around, she strongly insisted that he lay still while she summoned a nurse to come and look at him. Peter allowed his head to return to the softness of his pillow and listened as Elena shouted out very loudly for help.

A nurse quickly arrived in the room and checked Peter's vital signs and reported them to the doctor, who soon followed her into the room. Elena stood back from the bed as the doctor carried out further checks and asked Peter a number of questions, until he was eventually satisfied that Peter had suffered no further injuries. At that moment the doctor nodded to Elena to show that he was quite happy for Peter to be discharged.

When the doctor and the nurse left the room Elena pulled her chair back up to the bed and holding Peter's hand inquired how he felt. Peter told her that he was very sore and had quite a bad headache, but things could have been a lot worse. He lifted his head and asked Elena for more details about what had happened.

Elena told him that when the fight started she and Michael, plus his father, had ran outside the bar as quickly as they could and as a consequence, none of them suffered any injuries in their escape. George, her father, called the local police as soon as the fight started and it was not very long at all before the sound of the siren from their police car had been heard by the men attacking Peter. They looked at one another and one of them suddenly shouted out some instruction in a language that George did not understand and the men ran out of the bar and disappeared from sight.

Elena also informed Peter that when the men entered her father's restaurant, George noted that two of the men had American accents and two of them seemed to have what he assumed to be South African accents, when they conversed amongst themselves in English. George initially thought from their accents that the two men may have been South African, but occasionally they spoke in another language, which he believed was Hebrew. So he changed his mind and decided that these men must be Israeli. In any case, her father had not liked the look of the four men from the moment they entered the bar. They clearly treated him as though he was a lesser mortal to them and simply appeared to want to drink as much beer as possible in the shortest time. When asked, each one of them stated that they didn't want any food, they just wanted to drink. When Peter and Elena entered the restaurant with their Lebanese friends, the four men had quickly gone into a huddle and muttered amongst themselves with frequent glances towards the newcomers' table.

After Elena finished her background information, she began to chide Peter for starting the fight. She added that he could easily have ended up being crippled or worse, if the local police had not been so close to hand and were able to respond to her father's phone call as quickly as they had.

Peter nodded to Elena, but explained that the four men clearly had an issue with Michael and his father, probably just on the grounds that there was a civil war being fought in the Lebanon and if her father was correct in his belief that some of the men were Israeli, that may have been sufficient cause to incite them into causing the fight.

Peter also stated that whoever the men were, they had clearly been trained to high level in hand-fighting. Perhaps they were members of a karate or martial-arts club, or even ex-Special Forces.

Finally, Peter asked Elena to check with the hospital staff and see if he could be released, as he believed there was no more reason to keep him in the hospital and he was not sure if their health insurance policy would pay for all his treatment. In any case, he simply wanted to get home and back to work as soon as possible, as every day he was not taking diving parties out was costing them money.

Elena checked with the hospital staff and after some discussion amongst themselves, it was decided that it would be safe for Peter to be discharged from the hospital. The doctor told them that Peter had clearly suffered from some trauma to the head, which had caused mild concussion, but if he took it easy and followed the instructions on the packets of tablets he had prescribed for him, he should be up and back to work in just a few days.

Peter got himself dressed with the aid of Elena and they left the hospital and climbed into Elena's car for the 30 mile drive back to their home in Vrysoules village, where Franzie was waiting to greet them with frenzied enthusiasm.

Chapter 5
Friday, 14th August 1987

Peter woke up quite early that morning with Franzie licking his face energetically. He winced as he lifted his head to look at Elena, but found that she was already awake and out of bed. He gave Franzie a fond cuddle and ruffled his ears the way the little dog liked, before he reluctantly forced himself out of bed and enjoying the cool feel of the tiled floor of their bedroom, he walked over to their small kitchen and kissed Elena on the back of her neck.

Elena responded by looking at him anxiously and asking him if he thought it would be okay for him to be out of bed and walking about, after all he had been through just two days ago. Peter nodded his head and assured her that he was feeling fine and would certainly be okay to go back to the dive centre and start to pick up the business they so badly needed, to keep the bank manager happy. He poured himself a cup of strong coffee and as he snapped his early morning ration of prescribed tablets out of their packets, he swallowed them with a large mouthful of coffee.

After a few minutes, Elena reminded him that Ian Murray had looked after the diving party that had booked dives on the previous day and would gladly help them out with their customers on that day, if Peter did not feel he was up to diving. Peter thought about it for a moment or two and turning to look at her replied that all he had booked for that day was a "Suck it and See" session in the Pernera Beach Hotel, which was located just north of Fig Tree Bay. He felt he could easily cope with taking a few tourists and their children into their hotel's swimming pool and trying out breathing from a scuba set as he guides them around the pool.

Elena also mentioned that Michael had rung the dive centre late in the afternoon of the previous day and had enquired how Peter was progressing. She had assured Michael that Peter was on the mend and would be back to work as soon as possible. Michael had responded by asking her to pass on the best wishes of both himself and his father and also to tell Peter that he was very keen to do some more diving with him as soon as Peter felt up to it. Peter nodded and said that he really liked Michael and when he got to the dive centre, he would ring him and see if he could arrange for another dive in the next few days. Next he ate a quick breakfast, showered, dressed and when Elena finished tidying up the house and fussing over him, they both climbed into Peter's flatbed truck and drove over to their dive centre in Ayia Napa.

When Peter parked at the back of the dive centre, he lifted the barking, licking Franzie out and set him down on the ground. Franzie immediately expressed his thanks by staring at Peter with his adoring eyes and urinating over a small struggling Aloe Vera plant. Elena unlocked the doors of the dive centre and quickly went over to the diary to check that she was fully aware of all that had been booked for the day, which fortunately was just as Peter remembered, just the one booking for the "Suck it and See" session at the Pernera Beach Hotel.

As they were opening up the place, George spotted their arrival and was soon in the entrance of the dive centre, insisting that they both come over to his restaurant for something to eat. Peter smiled at Elena, knowing that they had no other choice than to enjoy a good Cypriot breakfast with her father.

After their breakfast Peter loaded up the back of their truck with full cylinders of air and a selection of face masks and other diving equipment and drove off to the Pernera Beach Hotel.

When he arrived at the hotel, he parked his truck and checked in with Charlie at reception. Charlie's real name in Greek was Haralambos, but many Greeks anglicised their names for the sake of the tourists. Peter next, with Charlie's permission, moved the diving equipment to the side of the hotel's swimming pool and finally erected his sign, offering free "Suck it and See" initial scuba diving experiences to the tourists around the pool. Very quickly several parents brought their delightful children over to the pool and Peter gave them a very quick briefing on the "Do's and Don'ts" of scuba diving in a swimming pool before he put the cylinders on their backs, fitted them with a suitable face mask before getting the children to drop on to their knees in the shallow end of the pool. Once he was happy that they were breathing successfully from the cylinder, he slowly pulled around in a short circle, then helped them to stand up again before declaring to the smiling parent that their child had the makings of a natural-born scuba diver.

It was slightly different with any adults who volunteered to have a go, for if they showed any signs that they would make a reasonable diver, Peter offered them an initial open water dive, which would only cost them the small sum of thirty-five Cypriot pounds. Luckily, Peter had a good day with four adults signing up for initial dives, which he arranged for the following morning. When it appeared that he was going to get no further takers, Peter packed away his diving equipment and drove back to the dive centre.

+ + + + +

It always amused Peter that when he drove up to the dive centre, Franzie would be running around in circles, yapping and wagging his tail so much that his balance often appeared to be compromised. As soon as Peter opened the door of the car, Franzie was bouncing up and down in sheer joy and excitement until Peter finally began to stroke him, which was clearly the closest thing to ecstasy that Franzie had ever experienced.

Elena came out of the dive centre, shaking her head at the antics of their little dog, as she helped Peter unload the truck. Peter told Elena that he had picked up four new divers from the "Suck it and See" and Elena noted the bookings in their bookings diary. She looked up and mentioned to Peter that she had received a phone call from Ian Murray, who had asked if Peter would give him a ring when he returned to the dive centre.

So, once all the diving gear was washed off and packed away, Peter picked up the telephone and dialled Ian Murray's dive centre.

Ian immediately asked how Peter was after his stay in hospital and Peter reassured him that he hadn't sustained any serious injuries and felt fit enough to get back to work again. Ian answered by saying that unfortunately, their chosen careers did not allow the luxury of taking too much time off work. Then he stated that the main reason he was ringing was to say that he had been diving with customers near to Cape Greco and that he had once again found fishing line leading up to what looked like suspicious packages floating near the surface. Ian had cut the line again and noted that the suspicious package slowly drifted away to the west, which would eventually carry it hopefully far out to sea. He added that he was really worried about what was in the package, but was even more worried that if it was anything to do with drugs or other criminal activities and the police got involved in an investigation, it could easily result in restrictions on diving in the Cape Greco area. This would seriously hurt their incomes, as all the best dives at that time were in the waters off Cape Greco, simply because the sea bed dropped away quite quickly from the Cape and offered the opportunities of diving at a good range of depths, without the need for boat diving.

Peter agreed with Ian about the impact a police investigation could have on their businesses and thanked him for the information about the floating package. He promised to keep a good look-out for other packages and after a few minutes of banter between these good competing friends he hung up and told Elena about Ian's warnings. Elena was equally worried about the prospect of police investigations into the floating packages and in a very strong tone she insisted that if Peter saw any of these packages, he was simply to ignore them and not risk getting involved with criminals.

Soon after the phone call, it was clear that there was going to be no new business for them that day, so they packed all the displays away, locked up the dive centre and drove back home to Vrysoules. On the way home, Peter stopped the truck at Litza's small supermarket in the village and bought some local bread, to go with the Tahini dip she would be making to accompany their evening meal.

Peter had to admit that he was pretty tired when they finally arrived home, but a quick cool shower soon restored his feelings and he thoroughly enjoyed their evening meal with its English and Cypriot touches. After watching an hour or so of television, to which he added the enjoyment of two large bottles of Keo beer, both Peter and Elena retired to bed and had a good night's sleep.

Chapter 6
Saturday, 15th August 1987

Peter and Elena arrived at the dive centre just before nine o'clock in the morning. They were not at all surprised to find Michael, standing by his car smoking a cigarette and playing with his Zippo lighter.

As Elena unlocked the door of the dive centre, Michael extinguished his cigarette, approached Peter and said, "Today I have nothing, so I think I will go diving with Peter."

Peter explained that at the moment the only booking he had was for him to take out four novice divers on their first open-water diving experience. But as Michael seemed perfectly happy to go out with him and the novice divers, Peter smiled and nodded at Michael and began to explain how he handled novice divers.

At a quarter to ten, Peter left Elena and Michael at the dive centre and drove off towards the Pernera Beach Hotel where he found his four novice divers waiting in the car park in front of the hotel. He put his best smile on his face and greeted them enthusiastically, pointing towards the sea and telling them that the morning was just perfect for them to enjoy their first open-water scuba diving experience. He checked that they all had a towel with them and that they were wearing swimming costumes under their outer clothes, before asking them to take their seats in the truck and setting off on his return journey to the diving centre.

When they arrived at the diving centre, he introduced them to Elena and Michael. Next Elena provided each of them with a form which she asked them to complete. The form started with the personal details of the customers, their names and addresses and finally asked them a series of questions regarding their health and fitness to dive. At the bottom of the form was a neat little disclaimer which required each customer's signature and showed that they were all willing to take on the open-water diving experience at their own risk.

Once Elena had checked to make sure that the forms were completed to her satisfaction, she asked if any of the customers would like a cool drink, which she gladly supplied to those who requested one before informing them that before they would be allowed to go diving, they must all be given a short lesson in how to breath air from a scuba diving cylinder and the "Do's and don'ts" of scuba diving.

Peter always enjoyed giving this short lesson and with the experience of delivering this presentation many times, he enjoyed adding little humorous touches to the lecture, which immediately put the novice divers at their ease. At the end of the lecture, he asked each of the divers a few questions to make sure that they all understood the important things which would keep them safe during their dive.

Then with the aid of Elena, he fitted each customer with a wet suit, face mask and fins and once again they climbed into Peter's truck for the drive to the dive site. Michael followed behind the truck in his car. Elena gave them a wave as they set off to the dive site, holding Franzie in her arms and waving his paw at the vehicles as he barked in disappointment at being left behind.

+ + + + +

After a short drive they arrived at Green Bay, which lies only just over a mile north of Cape Greco. The bay has a convenient parking area with a very small beach, which is easily accessible from the car park. Peter parked his truck just past the access point to the beach and when everyone had climbed out of their vehicles, he told them that he would give them a walking brief showing them where they would be diving. Peter led the novice divers and Michael to the short narrow path that was used to get down to the small beach and explained that caution was needed when wading out into the bay as there were rocks on the bottom that can prove tricky to walk over. With Michael bringing up the rear of the party he walked them along the rocks that formed the headland, pointing out to the party that the water gradually got deeper as the bay widened out towards its mouth. As they continued along the rocks Peter called out to a diving friend of his who was taking another party of tourists out into the bay.

"Is that Johnny Saunders?" He called out, "This is a bit better than swimming around in the public baths in Wanstead."

The sun-tanned blond haired head of his friend spun round and after a quick smile of recognition, John responded with a slightly rude gesture, before he returned his attention to the five young novice divers he was instructing.

Soon Peter, Michael and the novice divers were standing on the salt splattered rocks at the point of the headland and Peter pointed to where the rocks dropped off to the sandy bottom. Here he explained that if they were very lucky, they may meet up with one of the friendly green turtles that are sometimes seen in the bay.

Just at that moment one of the novice divers pointed out to sea and commented on a passing white hulled cabin cruiser, which was just passing the bay on a southerly course, saying, "That boat would make a good diving platform."

Peter followed his directing gesture and nodded saying, "That is a bit posh for around here. Normally, the only boats we see are the rather bedraggled local fishing boats. I wonder where he is off to?"

Peter turned back towards his truck and told the visiting divers that it was time to change into their swimwear and get into their diving equipment.

When each diver in turn was ready, Peter began to help them put their cylinders on their backs and finally, he helped them put on their weight-belts. Next he checked that each diver's pillar valve was correctly turned on and showed each diver that they had around two-hundred bar of air pressure in their cylinders, which would be more than enough for the dive he had planned for them.

At this point, Peter introduced the novice divers to Michael and explained that he was an experienced diver who would be coming along with them on the dive, but if they needed any help at all, they should ignore Michael and indicate to Peter with the shaking hand signal that they needed assistance. Finally, Peter picked up his Nikonos 4 underwater thirty-five millimetre camera and led the way down to the small beach.

Once everyone was safely down on the beach, he advised them once again to be cautious as they waded out into the sea as there were some rocks on the bottom of the bay, which could prove to be hazardous. Slowly they all waded out until the water was up to their chests, at which point Peter showed them how to spit in their face masks to prevent misting and helped them put their face masks on and check out their buddies to see that the face masks were correctly mounted and water tight. Once the depth of the water had reached their chests, Peter showed them how to put on their fins and when they were ready, helped each in turn to do so. When they were all kitted up and ready to go underwater, he instructed all the novice divers to put their Regulators into their mouths and drop down on to their knees so that they could get used to breathing off their own cylinder while under water.

Eventually, having made certain that they were all breathing confidently off their cylinders, he indicated that they should follow him and he began to lead the party down the gradually sloping sea bed into deeper water. Each of the novice divers soon began to feel more relaxed breathing underwater and Peter could tell that all four of the novice divers were really beginning to enjoy the experience of scuba diving.

At that moment Peter noticed that one of the female novice divers, who he had learned was called Janet, was having difficulty getting off the sea bed, so he finned across to her and added a small amount of air to her buoyancy aid, until she became more neutrally buoyant and was able to fin forward more easily. He also noticed that one of the male divers was a bit too buoyant, so he indicated to him that he should let a bit of air out of his buoyancy aid, which the novice diver successfully did and was then able to move forward more quickly than before.

Soon the diving party approached a group of large boulders, beyond which the sea bed quickly dropped down to a depth of around ten metres. Peter led the way for the novice divers with Michael bringing up the rear of the party. When they had all dropped down to the sea bed at ten metres, he encouraged them all to add a little bit more air to their buoyancy aids to compensate for the loss of buoyancy that came with depth. Then he grouped them all together and took two photographs of them all with his Nikonos 4 underwater camera.

Once the photo was taken Peter led the party into slightly deeper water, where there was a very large boulder around which there were many small fish. Once again, he posed the novice divers on the rock and took a few more photographs of them, surrounded by the brightly coloured sea wrasses, single spotted breams and red mullets, all of which seemed to use the large boulder as a meeting and grooming location.

Peter next indicated that each of the diving party needed to hold up their contents gauges, so that he could check that each of them had sufficient air for the remainder of the dive. When he had checked the air of each diver, he led them in a circular path around the big boulder before he started to take them slowly back into the bay at the end of their dive.

It was at this point that Peter noted that one of the female divers was having problems with one of her fins. The fin was obviously loose and as he watched her struggle to refit the fin, it dropped away from her foot. The lady diver began to reach down towards the descending fin, but with only one foot with a fin, she was having a lot of difficulty manoeuvring in the water. Peter immediately began to power-fin over to the diver in distress and soon had her missing fin in his hands. He quickly took hold of her foot and refitted her fin, but as he was doing this, he suddenly noticed that one of the male novice divers was also in difficulty and had taken out his Regulator from his mouth and was frantically attempting to swim to the surface. The male diver was obviously in a state of panic and Peter noticed that Michael was attempting to get to the diver in distress and assist him to get to the surface. Peter gave a very quick 'OK' hand signal to the lady diver who now had her fin correctly fitted to her foot and as her hand came up with the thumb and fore-finger touching, he finned as quickly as he could to the panicking male diver.

By the time Peter reached the panicking diver he had made it to the surface, ripped off his face mask and was loudly gulping in air in a very distressed condition. Michael had been the first to get to him and he was holding the panicking diver by his buoyancy aid as he attempted to calm down the struggling diver.

Peter instantly inflated the diver's buoyancy aid and taking control of the situation, instructed Michael to get back down to the other divers and lead them back into the safety of the bay. Sensing the fear of the novice diver, he took a firm grip of the novice diver and asked him what had happened to cause him to panic so much. The novice diver, whose name was Gareth, informed Peter between taking huge gulps of air, that he had suddenly found that no air was coming out of his cylinder and he had simply panicked when he thought that he may drown in the deep water. Peter reached around Gareth and put the problematic Regulator into his mouth and discovered that there was no air at all coming out of it from the cylinder. Peter changed the Regulator to his left hand and reached behind Gareth to the Pillar Valve on top of the cylinder. He was shocked to find that the Pillar Valve had somehow been turned fully off, thus preventing any air reaching the Regulator, but he kept the issue to himself for the moment, as he was conscious that Gareth may become distressed if he knew what the problem was. So Peter gently turned the Pillar Valve back to the 'ON' position and tested the regulator one more time. Content that the Regulator now delivered air correctly, he attempted to give it back to Gareth, but Gareth shook his head and gestured that he wanted to get back to the shore as quickly as possible.

Minutes later, when everyone climbed out of the water and walked the short distance back to Peter's truck, he gathered them all around and taking the bull by the horns, explained that for some unknown reason Gareth's air supply had become turned off. Peter stated that he had never known this ever happen to anyone before Gareth and he was at a total loss to explain how it happened. He helped Gareth to remove his air cylinder and showed the party how he had found the Pillar Valve turned off and just how hard it would be for this to happen accidentally. Stopping to emphasize the point, he repeated that he could think of no explanation at all as to how this had happened. Finally, he asked everyone to accept that this must have been a freak accident and he insisted that they must not to be put off any future diving, because of this odd incident.

The novice divers all nodded at the wisdom of Peter's words, which he acknowledged by inviting them to George's bar and restaurant, adding that he would gladly buy them their first drink. This seemed to put all thoughts of Gareth's problem behind them, so as soon as they were all dry, Peter drove them back to the dive centre, with Michael following in his car behind them. When they got back, Peter asked Elena to lock up the Dive Centre and afterwards join them for lunch next door in George's restaurant.

+ + + + +

As soon as they entered, George led them to his favourite table which was close to the bar and convenient to the kitchen. He graciously pulled back the chairs for the two lady divers, waited until everyone was comfortably seated before enquiring what each person would like to drink. With his order pad carefully noting the drinks, he moved back to the bar in order to leave his guests to continue their conversations.

This was very familiar territory for Peter and he soon found himself repeating his oft told stories about how he ended up running a scuba dive centre in Ayia Napa. Michael initially sat quietly listening to the conversations, but eventually Gareth began asking him questions about how he had learned to scuba dive in the Lebanon. Michael was slowly overcoming his shyness at conversing in English and after a few minutes became a quietly engaged participant in the conversations. Eventually, he even opened up about his early years as a member of the Christian minority community in the Lebanon and the difficulties they faced from the majority Muslim communities in their country. He explained that his Maronite Christian faith was much older than most other Christian communities and how many of their religious ceremonies pre-dated those of the later Roman Catholic and much later Protestant religions. It was soon clear to everyone that Michael was extremely proud of his Maronite Church and he explained how many aspects of this church could even be traced back to similar ceremonies in the old Jewish faith, from which the first Christian Apostles split in the early years of the Christian religion. Later he went on to explain the many different religious and political parties which had led to the Civil War, which was currently raging in his country and this had led to his family fleeing to safety in Cyprus.

As Michael continued with his story, George came back with the drinks and asked if anyone would like to order something to eat. George explained that his wife, Maroulla, was in the kitchen and she was an excellent cook.

Peter confirmed George's assessment of Maroulla culinary skills and informed the party that he highly recommended the Pork Chops, as George had a source that produced the biggest Pork Chops on the island. He also recommended that if someone didn't like Pork Chops, they should choose the halloumi and chips, which was one of Maroulla's special dishes. Next, George took all their orders and just as he was about to return to the bar, he asked if they would like some Tahini and olives as a starter, to which nearly everyone at the table readily agreed.

Soon the conversation naturally returned to scuba diving and two of the novice divers, Paul and Jenny, asked if they could do another dive with Peter, as they had really enjoyed their first scuba diving experience. Peter naturally agreed and asked them to liaise with Elena after their meal and assured them that he could take them on another very easy dive site just up the coast, which would be perfect for their second dive.

After a few minutes, George returned to the table with two bowls of Tahini sauce, a plate with a large sliced loaf of village bread, plus a plate full of small green Cyprus olives doused in lemon juice. Peter immediately broke off a large slice of the village bread and after dipping it into the Tahini sauce, took a large bite of the bread, exclaiming, "Sorry, but I just love Tahini sauce the way Maroulla makes it." He also added, "Come on everybody. If you don't grab it quickly, someone else will."

George interjected into the conversation and said, "Maroulla's Tahini is talked about all over the island, along with just how much she keeps me under the thumb. She is the real boss of the place for it is she who does all the accounts and handles all the cash. The restaurant simply wouldn't be able to run without her."

George was just about to turn away from the table when he suddenly stopped in his tracks and said, "By the way, there is a rumour going around the town that some drugs have washed up at Nissi Beach."

Peter's hand stopped mid-way to grabbing another slice of the village bread and he looked at George and asked, "What do you mean by washed up at Nissi Beach?"

George replied, "It was Maroulla who heard the rumour, as she was shopping in town this morning. I will ask her to come over and tell you what she heard." As he walked back to the bar, he shouted loudly for Maroulla to go over to tell Peter what she had heard about the drugs being washed up at Nissi Beach.

Maroulla, opened the door of the kitchen, behind the bar and began to walk over to the table that Peter and the divers were sat around. Maroulla was a short lady, who had clearly managed to keep her figure looking very trim, which she carefully managed to keep tucked into her black dress. Over her dress Maroulla wore a tidy Cyprus apron with olive motifs neatly stitched into the corners. Her hair showed hints of grey, but the feature that everyone noted was the pleasant smile that seemed to be a permanent feature of her strikingly attractive face.

As she approached the table, she smiled at Peter and Elena and once she had been introduced to the others, she flooded them with the warmth of her smiles. Peter soon asked her what she had heard and she started to tell them about the rumours going around the town's small market.

"I was talking to Maria about the wedding of her brother-in-law's second cousin's sister, when Sophia, who runs the cake shop, came up to us and told us that she had just heard that some drugs had been washed up on the beach at the end of Nissi bay. Evidently, one of the hotel cleaners was just finishing washing the floor of her corridor, when she noticed a large black bag, something like a dustbin bag, had been washed on to the beach. Her first thought was that there may have been fish inside the bag, as her husband has a fishing boat and he often uses that kind of bag to bring home the fish, but when she noticed that there were flat edges to whatever was inside the bag and her curiosity got the better of her, so she decided to investigate. Anyhow, as she approached the black bag she noticed that there was a long rope trailing out to sea from the bag, which seemed a bit strange. When she untied the rope, she opened the bag and to her surprise she noticed that there were some white cardboard boxes in the bag and also many plastic bags of white powder. All of which were securely wrapped up with many strips of grey plastic tape. The cleaner, whose name I think is Zoe, had seen many bags like those in the American movies that she likes to watch, so she ran back to the hotel and called the police on the telephone. Sophia said the police came very quickly and took the bag away and told her not to tell anyone about the drugs, as they are trying to keep the story out of the newspapers, just in case it puts tourists off coming to Ayia Napa for their holidays."

Peter looked to Elena and then to Michael and held one of his fingers to his lips, indicating that it would be best to keep quiet about what he and Michael had seen, when Ian cut the rope of the mystery floating object they had encountered on their dive at Tunnels the other day. He felt a little relieved when both Elena and Michael slowly nodded their heads to indicate that they noted his subtle gesture.

Soon Maroulla returned to the gossip she had heard at the market and was halfway through the problems Maroulla was having arranging the wedding of her brother-in-law's second cousin's sister, when George began to bring over their lunches. To everyone's relief, they politely began to ignore Maroulla's market gossip as they tucked into their lunches. Peter was pleased to note that all of the party clearly enjoyed their meals and everyone who had opted for one of Maroulla's Pork Chops, voiced their praises for the wonderful way she cooked this wonderful Cyprus specialty dish.

+ + + + +

After the meal, the party returned to the dive centre and after Elena booked the novice divers for their next dives, Peter drove them back to their hotel and afterwards returned to dive centre to find Michael and Elena deep in conversation as he entered the building. As soon as he sat down in one of the more comfortable chairs, both Elena and Michael turned their heads towards Peter and asked him if he thought the drugs that had washed up on Nissi Beach were connected to those the mysterious floating object that Ian cut loose on their dive at Tunnels.

Peter nodded and said he thought there was a very strong possibility that the two events were linked in some way. He went on to state that he thought it would be best if he gave Ian a call and explained what they had just learned. So he picked up the white telephone on the counter of the Dive Centre and dialled Ian's number. Ian answered the phone straightaway and Peter explained all about the rumour of the discovery of drugs on Nissi Beach and waited while Ian thought through the information. Ian replied by saying that he really didn't think it would be a good idea to mention to the police that they may have been involved in some way with the drugs and Peter agreed that it may have serious impact on their diving businesses if the police learned that they may have cut loose the drugs. Ian ended the conversation by saying that he would be staying away from the Cape Greco dive sites for a while, just in case there may be a police interest in any activities. Peter responded by agreeing in principle with Ian's concerns, but as nearly all his customers were in hotels around Cape Greco, it would be difficult for him to steer clear of the area.

After he had hung up the phone, Peter told Elena and Michael about his discussion with Ian and Michael asked him for a few more details, as he was keen to do some more diving in the next few days and had already booked up with Elena to go on a dive the next morning. Peter nodded and said that he thought that if they stayed away from the Tunnels area, which was really very near the tip of Cape Greco, everything should be okay. He added that he was glad that Michael had booked to go diving the following morning, as he already had a small party of British Army divers based in the Dhekelia Sovereign Base Garrison booked for a dive for Chapel Cave, which he thought would be ideal for Michael's next dive. Michael thanked Peter and picked up his shoulder bag and said "Good Evening" to Elena and Peter, before he headed out of the Dive Centre, lit up a cigarette with his trusty Zippo lighter and walked around to his car, which was parked at the rear of the building. Moments later, his red Nissan car drove out, with Michael cheerfully waving at them as he gave them a little hoot of his horn.

Peter turned to Elena and said, "Well, I think we have had enough excitement for one day, let's lock the place up and go home for a shower and a nice glass of Keo beer." Elena agreed, so they both began tidying up the dive centre and locked up the doors and headed out to their flatbed truck.

As they approached the truck, Peter asked Elena where Franz was, as he hadn't seen their little dog since they came back from their dive at Green Bay. Elena suddenly stopped walking and looked at Peter, saying that she hadn't seen him for some time either, so with slightly worried looks on their faces, they both began calling out for Franz and looking in his normal hide holes. But they couldn't find Franz and there was no response to their calls for him. Elena thought for a moment and said, "Mother." She quickly spun around and ran back to her parents' restaurant leaving Peter looking anxiously towards the rear entrance to her parents' bar. A few minutes later, Elena reappeared through the door to the kitchen of the restaurant shrugging her shoulders, with Maroulla and George emerging behind her with equally worried looks on their faces.

Elena and Peter, with Maroulla's help, spent over an hour searching for Franz before Elena suddenly let out a shriek and burst into sobbing and fell to her knees. Peter and Maroulla hurried over to her and they found her kneeling over the body of Franz, which was just inside a small clump of bamboo grass. Someone had clearly smashed poor Franz's head in with a large rock, which lay beside Franz's body and was clearly covered in the evidence of the assault.

Elena was simply heart-broken and she was sobbing very loudly as she tried to pick Franz's body up from besides the blood-covered rock. Peter helped her pick up their beloved dog's body and then took off his T-shirt and used it to cover the top half of Franz's body.

"Who could have done such a thing?" Cried Elena amongst her sobs, as she hugged Franz's body to her chest. Peter suddenly felt his resolve melt away and tears began to burn down his face as he tried to say something, but no words would come out of his mouth.

Eventually, Peter managed to regain control of his voice and he said quietly to Elena, "Let's take him home my love." To which, Elena just nodded and stood up with Franz held tightly in her arms and they began to slowly walk over to their truck.

+ + + + +

They buried Franz just in front of the fig tree at the back of their home in Vrysoules village, because it was his favourite place in their small garden. Franzie liked to chase the hornets that came to the tree to drink up the juices from the figs that became over ripe. He also habitually marked the ground around the tree with his special urine trademark.

Elena was devastated at the loss of Franz, particularly at the horror of how he had met his end. She repeated time and time again, "Just who could have killed poor Franzie in such a nasty way?"

Peter was also very upset by the death of Franzie, but in the back of his mind he knew that he had dives booked and he really didn't want to let down his customers, especially as they helped them to live such a good life in the place he adored. So he resolved to himself that at the earliest opportunity he would have to get back to work or he would have disappointed customers.

Later that evening, George and Maroulla came around to their home and while Maroulla sat with Elena and comforted her, George sat with Peter at the back of their home and they shared a few bottles of Keo beer.

George eventually brought up the subject of why Franz had been killed in such an awful manner.

"I have been thinking about the person who killed Franz and I have a suspicion that it may have been done by one of those four Israeli men that you had the fight with."

Peter thought for a moment or two and said, "You may be right George. But I don't think we have any evidence to prove that they may have been involved. In any case, would the police be interested in investigating the death of a pet dog?"

George replied, "I don't know Peter, but I will mention it to a friend of mine, whose son is a policeman and ask if they would investigate the death of a dog. But I think that those men may have been trying to send a message of some kind to you."

After chatting for another ten minutes, they went into the lounge of the house and rejoined Elena and Maroulla. Elena's eyes clearly showed that she had been crying again, but when the men entered the room she offered to make them coffee and they gratefully accept the offer, hoping that it will give Elena something different to think about.

Maroulla quietly told the men that Elena is very upset indeed by the death of Franzie, but hopefully her grief would make her so tired that she would quickly fall asleep as soon as she went up to bed.

Elena returned with the coffees and a few biscuits and George tried to move the conversation on to more pleasant subjects, including asking Maroulla if she needed anything from Larnaca, as he was thinking of driving across on Monday morning to get a few things for the restaurant from the Supermarket on the ring road of that city. Maroulla thought for a moment and said, "I will go to Larnaca. I need to visit my Auntie Phoebe, who has been a little bit ill over the last few weeks, so I could visit her and see if she needs anything. Afterwards I can drive across to the Supermarket and pick up what you need, if you give me a list. I always think that the melons they sell there, are the best on the island."

George nodded to the inevitable wish of Maroulla and said that he would write out a list before she went and added that it would very handy if she could fill up the car with petrol, because it was cheaper to get it from the Petrolina filling station on the way into Larnaca. It also meant that if Maroulla set out early, she could be back in Ayia Napa before their lunchtime trade came in for their meals in the restaurant, as Monday was often the easiest day of the week due to quite a few customers coming in after the weekend.

Chapter 7
Sunday, 16th August 1987

Just as Maroulla had predicted, Elena did fall asleep very quickly when she went to bed on the Saturday night. However, she did not sleep that well and woke up earlier than normal, causing Peter woke up soon afterwards, to the sound of Elena making coffee.

Peter quickly got out of bed and went to the kitchen, trying not to appear to be in haste to see Elena. When he entered the kitchen Elena turned and gave him a forced smile and asked him if he wanted any breakfast. Peter quickly realized that she did not want to mention Franz, so nodded and said he would really like something to eat and left the decision of what they would have for breakfast to Elena. She opted for a good old fashioned English breakfast and started to cook the bacon. Peter picked up his coffee and looked out of the window of the kitchen for a moment, until it hit him that he was looking at the fig tree where they had buried Franzie the evening before. He quickly turned his back to the window and asked Elena how she was feeling. She replied that she was feeling fine and perhaps they had better go down to the dive centre, as she couldn't remember if they had any diving booked for the day. Peter stated that he had already checked in his diary and there was no diving booked for the day, so they could do whatever Elena wanted, however she insisted that they should go down to the dive centre for at least some time to take advantage of an easy day and to tidy up some of the loose ends that they had been putting off during the week. Peter readily agreed, as he could see that it was Elena's way of getting away from their home for a time and putting Franz out of her mind, at least for a short while.

Minutes later they settled down to their breakfast of fried bacon, eggs and tomatoes with an additional top-up of coffee. When they had finished their breakfasts, they shared the task of washing up their breakfast things. Shortly afterwards, Peter got the truck out from its parking place alongside their home and they drove down to Ayia Napa.

When they reached the dive centre they both climbed out of the truck without saying a word. Elena unlocked the door to the dive centre and they both entered their second home in automatic mode. Peter checked the office diary to confirm that they had no bookings that day and moments later looked up when he heard Elena switch the electric kettle on to make coffees. A few minutes later, as he sipped his coffee, Peter reached behind the counter and picked up their little transistor radio, switched it on and tuned it with the frequency control, to get the best reception he could of the local British Forces FM radio station. He always liked to keep up with the news from home, even though he now considered himself a full-time Cypriot resident. He also liked the music they played and some of the saucy comments that the soldiers and their families included in dedications to the light pop music the station transmitted.

As he stood listening to the radio, Elena come back from their little kitchen area carrying two mugs of coffee. Peter thanked her and sat down in one of the chairs in their office and tried to make the morning as normal as he could.

Elena also drank her coffee in silence, but as she finished her cup, she suddenly stood up and walked over to the glass paneled front door of the dive centre, which she inspected closely and said, "Look at all these finger marks." Next moment, she spun around and went back to the kitchen area and opened the hot water tap to half fill a plastic bowl with warm water so that she could wash away the offending finger marks. Deeply engrossed in the task she didn't notice straightaway that George was stood on the other side of the door, until he gave a gentle knock on the glass. Elena jumped a little in surprise and opened the door as her concerned looking father entered the dive centre.

He was clearly struggling to find something to say, aware of the depressed atmosphere that Peter and Elena were giving off, so eventually he simply said, "Has the kettle just been boiled?"

Elena nodded and asked if he would like a cup of coffee. When George affirmed that he would, Elena went back out to the kitchen area and quickly made him his usual cup of coffee with its normal three heaped teaspoons of sugar.

While Elena was in the kitchen George quietly asked Peter if she was feeling alright. Peter nodded and told him that she was clearly trying to have a normal day and there had been no reference at all to Franz from either of them. George nodded to himself, took the mug of coffee that Elena handed to him and asked if it had the necessary three teaspoons of sugar in it and that it had been well stirred. When Elena confirmed that it was made to his specifications, he nodded and said, "Good."

Once he was sitting down in one of the comfortable customers' chairs George suddenly stated, "Oh, have you heard the latest news? The Ayioi Anargiroi Church burned down during the night."

Both Peter and Elena looked at her father in amazement. "How badly is it damaged?" Asked Peter.

"I don't really know," said George, "But the rumour is that the damage is pretty bad. It is only a small church, but it has a lot of wooden fittings and some very expensive icons and beautiful chairs in it. I really fear that if a fire took hold in there, the damage would have been quite extensive."

Peter thought for a few moments, before saying to Elena, "Perhaps we should go up there and see what has happened?" But George responded saying that he didn't think it would be a good idea to go there now, as the track leading to the church is only a rough track and if there have been fire engines going down there, they will probably have blocked up the track for some distance.

Elena next asked, "Was the fire an accident or was it arson?"

George simply answered that he thought it would impossible to tell at this time, but he was sure that the fire would be investigated and the cause identified fairly quickly.

Peter was beginning to feel a little guilty about the conversation they were having for although he now considered himself to be an active member of the Greek Orthodox Church, he was somehow pleased that such a tragic event had taken Elena thoughts away from poor Franzie and she was now taking a very active part in the discussion about the fire. He therefore tried as hard as he could to keep the conversation going by asking questions about the church and was surprised when George told him that he had heard that the church was built on such a remote point because it was thought that the church had originally been built on the remains of an ancient temple to the goddess Aphrodite, who was highly revered in ancient Cyprus as the goddess of love and the sea. Tradition had it that Aphrodite was born out of the foam of the sea at a place now called Petra tou Romiou in Greek and Aphrodite's Rock in English, which is on the eastern coast of Cyprus, approximately fifteen kilometres south of Paphos. Later she became one of the most important gods to the ancient city-states of Cyprus, with temples in many locations, but most of them in close proximity to the sea. Hence the temple to Aphrodite above Chapel Cave. With the coming of the Christian faith, it was believed that the old temple to Aphrodite had been destroyed by the new Christian converts and that some of the stones of the old temple had actually been used in the building of the new church of Ayioi Anargiroi. George interjected into the conversation to remind them that the Cypriot national holiday of Kataklismos was linked to Aphrodite, for although the holiday of Kataklismos was officially to commemorate the Flood of the Old Testament, the date of the holiday is widely believed to be that of the birthday of Aphrodite.

Elena and Peter soon found themselves telling stories about how they normally celebrated Kataklismos in the Cape Greco National Park, drinking lots of wine and beer and enjoying an open-air barbecue with Elena's family and friends. Neither of them mentioned that Franzie, their dog, always enjoyed the occasion and the extra portions of food he always received.

Just as their spirits seemed to be on a more cheerful level, the telephone chirped into life and when Peter answered it he found that it was Michael calling them to check that he had booked a dive for the following morning. Peter checked the diary just to make sure that the dive had been entered, before turning and looking pointedly at Elena, said he would just check with her to make sure nothing else had been booked and when Elena nodded her consent, he confirmed once more to Michael that the dive was booked and would take place. He added that he would be taking Michael for a dive on one of the most picturesque dive sites on the island, Chapel Cave, but added to Michael that they had just heard that the church on the site had burned down during the previous night. Michael sounded quite shocked and also intrigued about this, but when Peter tried to briefly describe what the rumours were, Michael stopped him by saying that he would have to end the call as his money was running out for the telephone call. So the call ended with Peter arranging to meet Michael at the dive centre at ten o'clock the following morning.

When George went back to his restaurant, Peter and Elena kept themselves busy cleaning diving equipment and checking that it all was in good working order and generally tidying up the place. Peter spent some time checking his favourite item of diving equipment, the Bauer compressor that he had bought cheaply from a diving outfit in Limassol which went bust, just as they were contemplating setting up the dive centre in Ayia Napa. The Bauer compressor could charge up three diving cylinders to the two hundred bar working pressure in just over fifteen minutes, which was as near ideal as they could possibly afford at that time.

When they thought that they had done all they could to keep the dive centre in a way that would attract future customers, they locked up its doors and walked the short distance to George's restaurant, for during the previous evening, Maroulla had invited them over for their lunch. Peter sat at his usual place by the bar, while Elena went into the kitchen to help her mother prepare the food. After half an hour, Maroulla and Elena emerged from the kitchen with Elena carrying Peter's meal of Pork Chops and chips, plus her meal of haloumi and chips, while Maroulla carried George's lunch of grilled red mullet and chips and her simple plate of Greek salad topped with Feta cheese and black olives.

As they ate their lunches they chatted about the small things that all families converse about, without anyone mentioning the awful death of Franz or postulating on who could have committed such an appalling act. When they had finished their meals and tidied everything away, Peter and Elena checked that the dive centre was fully locked up and drove back home to Vrysoules. After that they settled down in their home Peter noted that Elena would quite often look out of the kitchen window at the fig tree where Franz now lay, but they didn't discuss his death again during the remainder of the day.

Chapter 8
Monday, 17th August 1987

Michael was already waiting for them when Peter and Elena arrived at the dive centre just before 10 o'clock the next day. As on previous occasions, Michael was smoking a sweet smelling cigarette, which Peter noted came from a pack of American Camel cigarettes, which slightly jutted out from the breast pocket of his light summer shirt. He was also flicking open and closed his Zippo cigarette lighter which he was very proud to own. As he approached Peter, he greeted him by name, this always amused Peter as he pronounced his name as 'Pitta', which is the name of the bread used in Cyprus to envelop kebabs.

Peter responded to Michael's greeting by saying, "You are nice and early Michael, we will be able to get into the sea before any waves build up. We heard yesterday that the church above Chapel Cave burned down sometime during Saturday night and it would be interesting to see just how much damage there has been to the church. Then afterwards, we can go for a dive out of Chapel Cave, which I know you will enjoy."

Michael asked a few questions about the church and afterwards readily agreed to Peter's suggestion that they go for a dive from this special location, on the proviso that it is still accessible after the fire.

Elena meanwhile had unlocked the dive centre and helped Peter and Michael load up the truck with the required diving gear.

When Peter was satisfied that the truck carried all the equipment they would need for the dive, the two divers set off for Chapel Cave.

It didn't take too long before they cleared the growing town of Ayia Napa and headed up the hill towards Cape Greco. At the road junction, towards the top of Cape Greco, they turned down the narrow road leading to the radio station at the tip of the headland and after a short distance, they turned left off the road and headed down the worn dirt track to Chapel Cave. As they neared the site of the Ayioi Anargiroi Church the extent of the damage the fire had done to the church was immediately apparent. The church had been virtually destroyed. All that remained was the blackened shell of the church. The roof had collapsed inside the church and there was hardly any trace of the beautiful contents of the building, besides the blackened remains of the wooden support for the roof and the tiles that had fallen into the centre of the ruin.

However, there were two vehicles already in the car park when they reached it. One was a small fire brigade vehicle, parked in the car park above the remains of the church, with two black clad firemen sifting through the ashes, clearly trying to figure out what had caused the conflagration. The other was a small Japanese-made saloon car, covered in dust with a group of four local lads changing into swim suits.

Peter parked their truck as near as he could to the path leading down to Chapel Cave and after they had put on their wet-suits and diving gear he took Michael to the edge of the cliff above the cave and started to brief him about the dive they were about to undertake. Peter pointed out that once they had entered the water from the flat ledge infront of Chapel Cave, they would swim out away from the cave until they finally came to the drop off, where the rocky bottom ended and finally merged into the sand that would lead them to the much deeper waters. As he was briefing Michael, he noticed that Michael was being distracted by the four local lads, who they had seen in the small Japanese saloon car. The young men, by this time were enjoying the thrills of jumping off the cliff above the cave. Peter explained that the water just to the right of the cave was totally clear of obstacles and was more than deep enough for the lads to jump into without too much danger to themselves. They then watched the youths enjoying their screaming jumps into the water for a few minutes, before Peter finished his briefing and they climbed down the rugged path to the cave beneath them.

Once they were in the cave Peter could not resist telling Michael of the history of the church and the cave. He began with the story that the church had been built on the remains of an ancient Greek temple and continued with the church being built over it to Christianize the location. He also explained that over the years it appears that a number of hermits had lived in the cave, just staring out to sea and contemplating deep spiritual issues. Next Peter showed Michael around the interior of the cave and finally helped him climb down on to the flat ledge where they put their fins on. Before they entered the water, Peter did a final 'Buddy Check' on Michael and after giving him a hand signal signifying that all was 'OK', Peter stepped off the ledge and dropped into the clear water of the bay. After a second or two his head re-emerged from the water and after he had checked that his own gear was working fine, he indicated that Michael should follow him into the sea.

When both the divers were satisfied that everything was working as it should, Peter gave the hand-signal that they could start swimming away from the cave entrance. As always, Peter kept Michael on his right as they headed down over the rocky bottom to the deeper water ahead of them.

The black rocky bottom had many small holes in it, which always looked to Peter like small craters from heavy machine-gun fire. He smiled to himself as he remembered just how many times he had checked out all these holes, but never found anything more interesting than a decent Cowrie shell in any of them.

Once they were on the bottom, its features changed into much bigger boulders, before the boulders eventually ended and they dropped down another ten feet on to the sandy bottom with patches of Eel Grass. This slowly sloped away into the much deeper water of the bay.

At this point, Peter finned ahead of Michael and gave the 'OK' hand-signal to Michael, just to check that everything was still fine with his client and when Michael returned the signal, Peter indicated that they would now head northwards and gently pulled Michael in the direction he wanted them to take.

When they had finned along the bottom for a few more minutes a large metal anchor appeared infront of them. Peter pulled out his Nikonos 4 underwater camera and Michael, taking the message, finned over to the anchor and sat astride it. Peter took a few photos, then indicated to Michael that he should look behind the anchor and as Michael followed this instruction he became aware that there was a large field of broken pottery behind the anchor. Peter led the way to the broken pottery and Michael quickly realized that nearly all of the pottery shards were clearly the remains of broken amphorae, earthenware pots used in ancient times to transport wine, olive oil or any other produce, which could be put into these pots for transport purposes. Michael pulled several nice looking amphora handles out of the sand, but all of them were in a pretty broken state and clearly not worth the effort of retrieving, so eventually he came to the conclusion that it was best to just leave them all in situ in this field of artefacts.

Eventually, Peter tapped Michael on his shoulder and held up his contents gauge, which is the accepted way in scuba diving of asking the other diver to show how much air pressure the diver has remaining in his cylinder. Michael responded by showing Peter that he had just over one hundred bars left, to which Peter nodded and indicated with his hand that they should start back towards Chapel Cave. Michael replied with the 'OK' signal and they slowly started to work their way back to the shore.

By this time, Michael was totally at ease in the water and felt so relaxed that he was taking his time looking into every little cavity as they gradually moved into more shallow water. Next they went up over the large boulders until they eventually came back to the black rocky bottom with all the holes in it. By now they were only a matter of fifty yards from their exit point, so Peter was happy to let Michael have his fill of checking out these holes, which he knew contained nothing of interest. Peter merely rested with his hands comfortably held together around his waist as he checked his air pressure gauge once again and decided to let Michael continue his pointless search through the holes. However, after a few minutes, he realized that Michael was getting very interested in something he had seen in one of the holes. Michael was strenuously trying to get his right hand a long way into this hole and when he became frustrated that he couldn't reach the object of his endeavours, he would reposition himself and thrust his arm even further into the hole. Peter suddenly just had to know what Michael had seen, so he finned over to where Michael was by this time breathing air so quickly that large clouds of spent air bubbles were constantly issuing forth from his regulator. When Michael noticed that Peter was beginning to show an interest in his efforts, he consciously moved to block Peter's view of the interior of the hole and more energetically thrust his arm one more time into the cavity. Peter repositioned himself until he too could see into the hole and then, to his amazement, saw a large golden ring towards the rear of the hole that Michael was struggling with. Greed instantly surged through Peter's mind and he instantly joined the struggle to be the one who first managed to reach the ring. But when Michael became aware that he now had a competitor, he thrust his arm as far as he could into the hole, ignoring the pain of the sharp rock edges on his arm and was rewarded by finally getting his fingers to the ring and seizing it firmly in his fist, he pulled the gold ring out from the hole and rapidly swam up the slope to the exit point at the mouth of Chapel Cave.

Annoyed with himself that he had let Michael take the gold ring from the hole, Peter finned after him and when he broke through the surface of the water and was sitting in shallow water at the mouth of the cave, he asked Michael to show him the ring he had found. Michael, by this time was staring fascinated at the ring he now held so securely in his fist and ignored Peter's request.

Peter asked again if he could see the ring, this time in a little firmer voice, to which Michael answered, "Give me your troth that you will give it back to me straightaway."

Peter wondered where and how Michael had picked up the old English word 'troth', but readily agreed that he would give him back the ring, once he had inspected it.

Michael held back for a few more moments before reluctantly handing over the ring to Peter.

The first thing that struck Peter was the weight of the ring, it really was very heavy. This obviously indicated that in the pure weight of gold, this ring was clearly a very valuable object.

Peter noted that the ring had a square face on its front, with the image of flames standing out from the flat background. The maker of the ring had managed to get the flames to extend over the edge of the flat face and continued down one side. There were no other markings on the ring, so Peter thought it would be very hard to date the ring, but the one thing that still puzzled him was how on earth he had missed finding the ring before, in the countless times he had searched through every hole since he had first dived at Chapel Cave. By now Michael was growing anxious and holding his hand out to Peter for the return of the ring. Taking the hint, Peter handed it back to him and he once again looked at the ring adoringly.

"Do you think the ring is very old?" Asked Michael.

"I really don't know, but I suspect it is old. I don't think anyone would be able to afford to have such a heavy gold ring made nowadays." Replied Peter.

"Why is it not covered in rust and things?" Said Michael.

"I just don't know that either." Peter responded, "I only know that I have heard that gold doesn't get affected by concretion, like other metals do."

"So it could be very old?" Was Michael's final question.

This triggered a thought in Peter's head and he replied, "Actually, I think it is really old. So I think the only proper course of action for you is to take it to the Department of Antiquities in Larnaca. They should be able to date the ring and it is a legal requirement for all ancient artefacts to be handed over to them. It is illegal in Cyprus to keep any ancient items found on land or in the sea."

Content with this little act of revenge, Peter took off his fins and led the way back to the car park, where they took off their diving equipment and loaded it all into the back of the truck. Next they made sure that they were dried off and put their normal clothes, back on before they set off on the return journey to the dive centre.

Both of the divers were quiet on the drive back, but just as they were driving down the hill into Ayia Napa, Michael suddenly announced to Peter that he would take the ring to the Department of Antiquities as soon as he got back to Larnaca. Peter congratulated him on his decision and assured Michael that it was the right thing to do.

When they got back to the dive centre, Peter was surprised to find that Elena was not in the office. He unlocked the place with the spare keys he kept on the truck's key ring and unloaded the diving equipment with Michael's help. When everything was unloaded, he took the forty Cyprus pounds payment from Michael and put the notes into the cash box, which they kept locked in one of the drawers beneath the counter in the office. Michael asked if he could book another dive for the next day, which Peter gladly accepted, saying that he knew of another dive just beneath the headland of Cape Greco, that was known by all the local divers as Canyon. He followed on by advising Michael, that the climb down into the Canyon was a little bit of a struggle, but the Canyon quickly led divers out into thirty metres of water and the rays that are often seen on this dive are really something to write home about.

Michael finally shook hands with Peter, after thanking him for the best dive of his life. He also reassured Peter that he would take the ring to the Department of Antiquities in Larnaca, before he walked out of the dive centre to his car and drove off up the hill. Peter, by this time, had been worrying in the back of his mind why Elena had so unexpectedly left the office without leaving a little note to him explaining why she had left. So he decided to just walk the few paces down the road to George's bar and ask if he knew what had happened to Elena. When Peter was a few paces from George's bar he saw that the entrance door to the bar was closed, which was very strange at that time of day and he noted that there was a 'Closed' sign on the door. He also checked the little bit of open land behind the building and discovered that George's car was not there.

By this time, Peter was getting really worried, so he went back to the dive centre and rang George's home phone. After quite a few minutes of ringing, George answered the phone and from the sound of his voice, Peter immediately knew that something bad had happened. Suddenly, Elena was on the phone asking if she could help. Peter asked her if everything was OK, to which she just burst into sobs as she told him that Maroulla had been found dead in the burning wreck of her car. Peter simply told her that he was on his way home, slammed the phone back on the cradle and ran out to his truck which he started and then drove out of Ayia Napa as quickly as he could.

+ + + + +

Peter arrived at George's house after a very fast drive along the treacherous roads from Ayia Napa. He parked the truck as close as he could to the house, as there were already some vehicles already parked in front of the house. Seconds later he ran into the house and was met by Elena as she rushed towards him and fell into his arms sobbing very heavily.

George was sitting in his normal soft chair talking to their local Greek priest, Father Loucas. George was sipping at a very large glass of Cyprus brandy and looked at Peter with tear-filled eyes.

His eyes told just how much George was suffering and Peter noted that suddenly he looked a very old man.

Peter asked Elena what had happened and through the sobbed tale that Elena told him, he discovered that the local Ayia Napa Police had turned up at George's bar and after checking that they were talking to the husband of Maroulla, which they already knew as both were well-known to the police, they informed George that Maroulla's car had been discovered burning by the Sovereign Base Area (SBA) Police Force, who are responsible for the road leading from the Ayios Nicholaos British Army Base to the Garrison town of Dhekelia.

The car had been found just off the road, which skirted around the abandoned town of Akhna, where there was a sharp right-hand bend at the bottom of a small valley. There were no clues as to why Maroulla's car had come off the road, but the incident was being investigated by the SBA police with the cooperation of the local Greek Cypriot police force.

As Elena ended her sobbed account, Father Loucas, who was still sitting by the side of George, called Peter over to him with a subtle gesture of his fingers. Peter managed to get Elena to move towards the chair where her father was seated with the priest. When they were close to the chair, George raised his head just enough to look at them and tried to say something, but changed his mind and merely shook his head at them, indicating that he simply could not speak, before he dropped his head back down on his chest.

Father Loucas turned and looked up at Peter and with his eyes signalling that he needed help with George. Peter managed to free himself from Elena's grip and knelt down by George, taking a gentle but supportive grip of the old man's arm. George looked into Peter's eyes, but only silent tears ran down his face. This time it was Peter's turn to be speechless. All he could do was tighten his grip of George' arm in a silent expression of compassion. As Peter was holding George's arm, Elena knelt down by his side and putting her arms around her father's head, hugged him as tightly as she dare.

Father Loucas stood up from his wicker-bound seat and nodded his head to one side indicating that he would like to say something to Peter, who in turn straightened himself up and they moved a few feet away from George.

When Father Loucas considered they were just outside the ear range of George and Elena, he whispered to Peter that the SBA police had found Maroulla in her burned out car on a bend near Akhna. Peter nodded and said that he had already heard that, then he asked the priest if he knew any other details of the accident. Father Loucas shook his bearded head and said that the police were still investigating the incident, turning his face to look directly at Peter, he looked into his eyes and said, "George keeps mentioning something about four Israelis. Have you any idea what he is trying to tell me?"

Peter replied by saying, "I got into a fight recently with four men, who George thinks were Israeli, but I haven't heard anything other about them, unless you count the rumour that they were somehow linked to the package of drugs which were washed up on Nissi beach."

"Do you think they could have something to do with what has happened?" Asked the priest.

"I honestly don't know." Said Peter, "But they certainly looked a mean bunch of men on the one occasion I did see them. The one that I fought with really knew how to fight as he put me in hospital in very short order."

Father Loucas followed on by asking, "Should I mention it to the police?"

"I think it is certainly worth mentioning. I would also tell them that our little dog Franz was viciously killed by someone only a few days." Answered Peter.

They both looked back at George and Elena and after a few moments, Peter could not resist kneeling down again by Elena and holding his beloved father-in-law and wife in his arms.

Father Loucas looked down on them with his soft gentle eyes and bowing his head, he said a silent prayer for them, crossed himself and said Amen.

Eventually, people began to make their excuses and drift away from George's house, until only Father Loucas, Peter and Elena were left to comfort and support George. Peter offered to make George something to eat or drink, but all George could do was shake his head and point to the untouched glass of brandy by his side. Father Loucas later made his apologies, stressing that if anyone needed any help or support he would was perfectly prepared to return at any time. Before he left the house he tapped George on the back, shook hands with Peter, gave Elena a little hug and with a final goodbye, he set off home.

It was only after the priest left that George finally managed to express himself in words, when he finally said in a trembling voice, "I will be alright now, Elena, you get yourself off to bed and I will see you in the morning."

Elena told him that she just couldn't leave him in the state he was in, but George simply stood up and gently began to push them towards the door and Peter and Elena gradually took the hint and reluctantly found themselves outside the door of George's house.

They looked at each other and Peter put his arm around his tear-drained wife and guided them back to their own house. Then he managed to get her to climb the stairs to their bedroom and without saying a word, they both undressed and got themselves ready for bed.

As they lay on their soft mattress, Elena turned to Peter and said in a trembling voice, "Why is life so hard, Peter?"

Chapter 9
Tuesday, 18th August 1987

Neither Peter nor Elena slept much that night, each lying in bed listening to the breathing of the other, hoping that they were getting some sleep, but very conscious of the fact that neither of them was. Eventually, the light of dawn began to sneak into their bedroom around the blinds in their bedroom windows.

After what seemed like hours, Peter turned his head towards Elena and seeing that her eyes were wide open, he asked her if she would like a cup of tea. Elena slowly turned her head, so that she faced him and gently nodded, saying, "If you like."

Peter kissed her on the cheek and climbed out of bed, went down the stairs to the kitchen and put on the electric kettle. He took two mugs out of the cabinet behind him and added a tea bag to each mug and when the kettle reached boiling point and switched itself off, he added the steaming water to their drinks. He was just about to carry the drinks up to the bedroom, when it dawned on him that it would be nice if he added two biscuits to the tray he was holding, which he did and carried the tray up to Elena. When he reached the bedroom he found that Elena had not moved while he had been in the kitchen, so he quietly put her mug of tea and biscuit on to the Lefkara-laced top of her bedside table. A few moments later, he put his mug and biscuit on to his bedside table and climbed back into their bed.

The fan in their ceiling continued to waft a gentle cooling breeze down on to the pair of them as they silently drank their tea and munched their biscuit. Peter tried to think of something encouraging to say, but totally failed to find anything appropriate, until Elena turned her head towards him and asked, "What should we do now?"

It was only when this question was asked of him that Peter remembered that Michael had booked a dive for that morning, so he sat up in bed and turned to look at Elena and said, "I am really sorry, darling, but it has just dawned on me that Michael has booked a dive for this morning."

As Elena started to say something, he interrupted her by saying, "I know that I simply have other things to do now, but I will have to go down to the dive centre and be there to explain what has happened when he turns up."

Elena closed her mouth and turned her head back so that she was once again facing the ceiling fan, then she slid herself back under the thin cotton sheet which had overnight become her security blanket.

Peter checked the time and noted that it was still only just gone six o'clock in the morning, so he too pulled the sheet over him and rolled over on his side with his back pressed up against the reassuringly warm back of his beautiful wife, as he feigned that he was trying to drop off to sleep again.

At nine-fifteen that morning, Peter was ready to drive down to the dive centre to meet up with Michael and tell him that, unfortunately, there would be no diving on the day.

Before he left, he checked with Elena that she was content with him leaving her on her own to care for George and when she nodded with a weak smile on her face, he walked over to their truck, started the engine and with a final wave to the house, began the familiar drive back down to the dive centre in Ayia Napa.

When he arrived at the office, he parked the truck, opened up the dive centre and spent a little time sat waiting for Michael to arrive.

Shortly before ten o'clock, Peter recognized Michael's car as it came along the road to the dive centre. He waved to the car as it pulled up, walked over to it and knocked on the passenger window. Michael leant across the passenger seat and wound down the window sufficient for Peter to bend down and inform him that due to a death in the family he was very sorry but he would have to cancel the planned dive. Michael stated that he was truly sorry to hear that someone had died and after a few moments politely asked if it was anyone he knew. When Peter told him that it was Elena's mother, Maroulla, who had died, Michael looked suitably shocked and expressed his profound sympathy for what had happened, asking Peter to pass on all his regret to George and Elena. He added that he completely understood the situation, but as he would be going back to Lebanon on the coming Saturday, if Peter found it possible to fit it another dive before he left, would he please let him know by telephoning him on this number, which he wrote on the reverse of scrap of paper that he found in the glove compartment of his car. Just before he left Michael again begged Peter to pass on his sympathies to Elena and George. Then Peter stood back from the car, allowing Michael to start up the engine again and begin the drive back towards Larnaca.

When Michael's car disappeared from sight Peter locked up the dive centre, walked back to the truck and in turn, began his drive back home to Vrysoules.

When he parked the truck in front of their home, Peter walked up to the door and entered their home, calling for Elena, but was not surprised to find that she was not there, so he closed the door and walked down to George's house, where as expected, he found Elena sitting by the side of George, as he drank a cup of coffee.

They both looked up at Peter, as he approached them and although he wanted to ask how things were with both of them, all he found he could do was tell them that he had met up with Michael, whom he had told that there would be no diving that day.

Both George and Elena merely nodded in response and then the conversation had completely dried up. Peter simply did not know what to say, so he pulled up another chair, into which he lowered himself and joined in the silence of the two people who were so crucially important to him.

After some time, there was a soft knock on the door, to which Peter pushed himself out of his chair, to discover that Father Loucas was waiting on the doorstep. Peter immediately invited him in and thanked him effusively for his help comforting George on the previous evening. The priest brushed off Peter's thanks, telling him that not only was it his job to help members of his flock in times of trouble, but he would have done all he could in any case because George was a good friend of his and he always helps his friends.

Peter led the way to where George was sitting with Elena stroking his arm and with an unexpected change of voice, Father Loucas said, "George, there is nothing you can do at the moment for Maroulla, as she will have to remain in Larnaca while the police undertake their investigations. So you my friend, need to get back to your business. Otherwise, you will be losing customers and that is something no Greek business man is willing to do."

George looked at the priest in surprise and for the first time since the tragic news broke, he managed a bit of a smile and said, "Thank you, Father. I think I needed that bit of advice."

Slowly George pushed himself out of the chair, with a bit of help from Elena, he walked out to the kitchen, put on his apron and jacket and announced that he was going down to his restaurant to get back to work.

Elena immediately offered her help in running the kitchen, which George wordlessly agreed to, with a nod of his head.

Peter, being taken a little by surprise at the sudden change of mood, was a bit slow in reacting, but eventually offered to drive everyone down to Ayia Napa, before looking back at Father Loucas, who merely nodded his head with a warm smile and gestured to them that they should get on their way.

+ + + + +

Hardly before they knew it, they were pulling up infront of George's restaurant. George led the way to the door, which he unlocked and Elena and Peter followed him in to his business. George went behind the bar and switched on the lights, fans and other electrical functions. Soon he was busying himself with setting up the restaurant for his first customers of the day. Elena went naturally into the kitchen, where she has spent many happy years helping her mother prepare the meals and snacks and quickly got things organized in a way that suited her cooking habits.

Peter watched them both going about their tasks as if nothing had happened and decided that it would be appropriate if he responded by opening up the dive centre, so he told Elena that he would opening up, kissed her on the cheek and in a slightly bewildered manner walked the few paces up the road and unlocked the building. When he reached the dive centre, he remembered that it was only an hour or so since he had told Michael that there would be no diving that day, so he took out the scrap of paper on which Michael had written this number, which he then dialled and waited for a response. Luckily, Michael quickly answered the call and Peter began telling Michael of all that had happened to them since yesterday. Peter quickly got back to business, saying that as things were now more or less back to normal, would Michael like to go diving at the Canyon the next morning, which would be Wednesday, 19th August.

Michael jumped at the chance of another dive, for he pointed out to Peter that he was planning to fly back home to Beirut on the coming Saturday, as he had business there that needed his attention. Peter wrote the booking in the dive centre's bookings diary and thanked Michael for his understanding and ended the call.

Peter spent the rest of the afternoon, simply hanging on in the dive centre, while he let things settle down to as normal as possible in George's bar.

Several local people came in to offer their condolences to Peter and the family and he noticed that even more went in to George's bar to speak personally with George and Elena.

Finally, at five o'clock, having had no other bookings that afternoon, he closed the dive centre and walked back down the road to sit with George and Elena. When he opened the door to the bar, he was very surprised to see that the place was just about packed with people, expressing their sympathies by reminiscing countless tales about Maroulla, which were accompanied by many healthy glasses of Cyprus brandy or Keo beers. Hence it was quite late before Peter managed to get George to close his restaurant, before he drove the three of them back home to Vrysoules village.

When they got home, he let Elena take a slightly tipsy George back to his house and put him to bed, where he quickly fell asleep. As soon as Elena heard her father snoring she checked that all was secure in his house, before she walked the few paces back to their own home for the night.

Chapter 10
Wednesday, 19th August 1987

Once again, Michael was waiting for him when Peter arrived at the dive centre just before ten o'clock in the morning, but this time Michael was holding a large bunch of flowers in his arms. Peter waved at him as he drove behind the dive centre to his usual parking place, near the rear door so that he could easily load diving gear on the back of the truck.

As Peter approached him, Michael handed him the bunch of flowers with a compassionate look on his face as he said, "Please give these to George and Elena and tell them I was so sorry to hear of the death of Maroulla."

Peter expressed his sincere thanks as he accepted the flowers, but mentally made a note that he may slightly modify Michael's sentiments when he gave them to George and Elena. He then opened up the dive centre and put the flowers into a bucket of water to stay fresh until he took them home with him at the end of the day. After that he explained to Michael that he planned for them to dive at an exceptional dive site called the Canyon. This site was right at the southern edge of the high headland of Cape Greco. Although the site was normally accessed by motor vehicle, it really was a tricky place to get to and normally only four-wheel drive vehicles could make it there, but his faithful old flatbed truck had made it successfully there many times, so he had great confidence that it would do it again that morning.

Michael replied that he was really looking forward to the dive as Elena had mentioned it several times and he knew it was very popular with visiting divers. He added that as he would be going back to Lebanon on Saturday, he was sure it would be a suitable dive for his final dive on this trip to Cyprus.

Twenty minutes later, when the two of them loaded all the diving gear that Peter selected as the most suitable for the dive, on to the back of his truck and finally locked up the dive centre, they started the drive to the Canyon dive site.

After five minutes, they were driving on the familiar road out of Ayia Napa, heading up the hill towards the headland of Cape Greco, but this time after another ten minutes they turned right on to a well-worn dusty track that headed towards the sea. After a few more minutes, they reached the top of a small gradient and ahead of them was the beautiful bay which was famous for the sea caves in the sandstone cliffs that surrounded it. However, instead of driving straight on down to the bay, Peter turned left on to a very narrow track that headed towards the shoreline surrounding the Cape Greco headland. The track really was hard to follow and Peter was taking a lot of care to keep clear of the many large rocks that were exposed along the track. The next ten minutes proved to be some of the most adventurous driving that Michael had ever experienced. He found himself holding strenuously on to the dashboard of the truck and the hand of the door, looking seriously at the rocky outcrops that Peter was navigating around and the stressed face of Peter, who kept assuring him that his trusty truck could handle rocky paths, which even Cyprus donkeys refused to go down. Finally, Peter tugged the steering wheel of the truck hard around to the left and brought the truck to a halt on a small area of flat rocks with the sea perilously close on their right side.

"Well Michael, here we are." Said Peter.

With no sign of reluctance, Michael opened the passenger door of the truck and climbed out with a huge sigh of relief, saying, "I never imagined that the road would be that bad. I have never been along a road like that before. But where is the Canyon?"

Peter responded by simply telling Michael to follow him and to Michael's amazement, they only walked a few paces forward before their eyes took in a narrow split in the rocks at the bottom of the headland that soon widened into a ten feet wide outlet to the sea.

"There you are Michael." Said Peter, triumphantly. "Let me introduce you to the Canyon."

Michael carefully stepped forward a few more paces until he was looking down into the Canyon, watching the incoming waves surge back and forth over the rocky bottom of the split in the rocks.

"How do we climb down there?" He nervously asked Peter.

"If you look just down here, you can see there are a few foot holds. Once we are all kitted up, I will lead the way and you will see that it isn't too bad." Replied Peter, reassuringly.

He led the way back to the truck, where they got changed into their wetsuits and put on their diving equipment. When they were both ready for the dive, Peter looked at Michael and noting that he still looked somewhat anxious, he playfully punched him on the shoulder and told him that it wasn't as bad as it looked and led the way to the narrow descent path to the Canyon. There he patiently pointed out the foot holds once more, as he agilely demonstrated how to climb down into the Canyon. After a few moments of hesitation Michael nervously followed until they were both standing on a sloping rock just above the sea. Peter leant against the rock wall and pulled on his fins, then he spat in his diving mask to help prevent it from steaming up, before he fitted it to his face, put his regulator in his mouth and with a confident 'OK' hand signal to Michael he stepped out into the sea.

Michael watched until Peter's head popped back up in the sea and watched carefully as Peter swam a few feet away from the rocky ledge, before turning back and gesturing for Michael to follow his example. Michael took a deep resigned breath, put on his fins and mask in the same manner as Peter and with his regulator gripped tightly in his mouth, he also stepped out into the sea and finned the few feet to move alongside Peter.

When he felt confident that Michael was ready to start the dive, Peter gave him one more 'OK' hand signal and when a similar hand signal was returned, Peter lifted up the hose of his buoyancy compensator and let all the air out of his device until he gently began to sink beneath the waves. Once again he was watching all the time to make sure that Michael followed his example and when they were both just below the surface, Peter turned and headed out into the open sea.

As they finned out of the narrow rock opening, the bottom dropped straight down to some twenty metres of depth. Michael noted that the visibility was exceptional, with the crystal clear water only slightly obscured by the small bubbles in the water which were being generated by the waves breaking on the rocky headland.

Both divers dropped down to some fifteen metres below the surface and when Michael responded positively to yet another 'OK' hand signal from Peter, they both finned out further from the rocky shore until they were finning along about twenty-five metres below the surface, with the bottom below at thirty metres.

After a few minutes, Michael felt Peter tap his arm and when he looked at Peter, he saw that he was pointing to a patch of sand just ahead of them on which two Roughtail Stingrays were basking in the warming rays of the sun. Peter tapped Michael's arm again and indicated to him that the rays were dangerous by drawing his thumb across his throat and indicated that they should take a circular path around the rays which would lead them further to the east.

Soon Michael noticed that there were many more rays just ahead of them, so it was his turn to tap on Peter's arm and point in the direction of the rays.

Peter nodded his head and finned slowly ahead with the relaxed fin strokes of a very experienced scuba diver. They continued their way along the shoreline, noting the various different types of fish as they went.

After some twenty minutes in the sea, Peter finned until he was just ahead of Michael again and this time held up his contents gauge to show that he had just less that one hundred bars of pressure left in his cylinder. Michael checked his gauge, then showed it to Peter, for it was showing that he was down to just over eighty bars, to which Peter indicated that it was time they turned around and started to head back towards their exit point. Michael nodded to Peter and they both turned round and started to fin back to their exit point with the shore line now some fifty metres to their right.

As they were finning along, Peter started to detect the throbbing of a boat engine, which sounded as if it was heading towards them. After a few minutes, he became aware of a shadow moving over the sand beneath them. When he looked up he saw the blue bottom of some sort of motor boat, moving over and ahead of them, but as this was such a popular route for boats to cruise around, he didn't think too much about its presence, as it was probably just another gin palace with a fat rich Greek owner at its helm.

After a few more minutes he recognised the rocks leading to their exit point in Canyon, so he attracted Michael's attention and led the way into the narrow rocky channel. When he was able to stand on a rock with the sea around his chest, he took his fins off his feet and pulled himself out of the water on to the rocks above.

When he felt secure, he turned around and helped his friend out of the water and after a few enthusiastic comments from Michael about the dive, he led the way up the short climb out of the Canyon.

Once again, Peter turned back to Michael and helped him out of the rocky gorge. They then turned to lead the way back to their truck, when suddenly, two men stepped out from behind some large rocks with sub-machine guns pointing in their direction.

Peter instantly recognized the men as two of the four men who had initiated the fight in George's bar. Both Peter and Michael stopped walking and stood there, dripping wet holding their diving fins and face masks in their hands, with the weight of their diving gear pulling down on their shoulders.

One of the men with a sub-machine gun, which by now Peter had identified as the Uzi 9mm weapon, commonly used by the Israeli Armed Forces, indicated with the barrel of his gun, that they should put their hands up and turn to face the rocky face behind them.

Both the divers followed the instructions and dropped their fins and masks, then with their hands raised above their heads, they turned and faced the rocks. As they stood with their hands raised, one of the men, keeping well out of the line of fire of his accomplice, reached around each diver in turn and released their weight belts and buoyancy compensators. When they were loose he slid them off their shoulders and cleared them away from behind them.

Next, he pulled each diver a few feet backwards, until he could move infront of each man and proceeded to fasten their hands together with strong-looking nickel-plated steel handcuffs.

Peter and Michael exchanged glances to one another and Peter noted that even though he felt surprised and helpless, Michael looked absolutely terrified at what was happening to them.

Peter also noted that so far the two armed men had not spoken a word to each other and yet they had easily apprehended the two divers in a very professional manner.

The apparent leader of the two men gestured with the barrel of his weapon that the two divers should move back to face the rocks again and as they did so, he pulled out a small VHF transceiver and in a language that Peter recognized as Hebrew, he made a short broadcast on the radio. Moments later, a short hiss of static came from the transceiver followed by a single word acknowledgement from the other end of the communication path.

A few minutes later, Peter and Michael began to hear a motor boat approach towards them. Soon the motor was throttled back and Peter could imagine the skipper of the vessel reverse the vessel's engines so that he could hold it fairly stationary just off the rocky shore.

One of the gun men moved into the eye sight of the divers and he gestured that they turn around and start walking towards the sound of the vessel. As Peter led the way over the rocky ground he caught sight of the vessel ahead of them, which he realized was the white motor boat that he had seen a few days ago when he took the four novice divers for their dive in Green Bay.

On the motor boat, another of the four men who he had originally met in George bar, was extending a boarding plank between the rocky shore and the motor boat. When the man felt that the plank was secure, he released it and reached back behind him to a vicious looking pump-action shot gun, which had had its barrel sawn off to make it easily concealable. He pulled the shot gun forward and indicated to the two divers that they should use it to board the motor boat. The shot gun looked old and very much used, which indicated to Peter that this gang of men were well versed in violent and bloody operations.

Peter looked back at the lead gun man who once again gestured with his weapon that they should use the boarding plank to climb aboard the motor boat. As he did so, the lead gun man pulled out a pistol from behind his back and held it to Michael's head, warning Peter that if he tried to escape by diving in the sea, Michael would bear the consequences.

Peter simply accepted his fate and walking carefully down the boarding plank to ensure he kept his balance. At the end of the plank Peter climbed down into the motor boat, where he was soon joined by Michael and the two gun men. The gun men next indicated that Peter and Michael must sit down on the bench seat at the back of the open deck of the motor boat.

The boarding plank was quickly pulled back into the vessel and the skipper reversed the boat away from the rocky shore and headed out from the headland on a southerly course. After about ten minutes they were roughly two miles out from Cape Greco, when the helmsman pulled the throttle back and slowed the motor boat down until it was just gently drifting on the slow-moving current.

While they had been cruising away from the shore, Peter had been mentally busy trying to take in what had happened to them and anything in their immediate vicinity that could be of help to them in their seemingly dire predicament. He was now absolutely sure that the men who had taken them prisoner were indeed the four men with whom he had fought in George's bar a week earlier. The only one he hadn't seen, was the man who had beaten him in the fight, but as there was a flying bridge above them where the helmsman was navigating the boat, he assumed that the missing man was upstairs on the flying bridge.

Peter also noted that just to his right there was a large metal wrench, lying discarded in the corner of the floor of the decking. If he had the chance to get hold of this wrench, even with his hands secured with handcuffs infront of him, it would make a pretty deadly weapon.

At that moment, his army training kicked in and as he had been trained in the Army, he started looking for his Plan B. As their captors had been content to let them see their faces, Peter was working on the assumption that they would not be allowed to live and tell their tales to anyone. This made his prime concern the fact that he simply had to survive so that Elena and George, the two most important people in Peter's life, would not have to suffer any more pain and sorrow. Cautiously, he looked around for another way out of this situation and in moments he came to the conclusion, that although the boat he was in was about a mile from shore, if he didn't get the chance to use the heavy wrench to incapacitate his guard, he could always just stand up and dive into the sea and swim back to shore, For even with his hands in handcuffs he was sure he could make it back to shore.

As he continued to look around for other chances of escape, he heard footsteps on the roof above his head, which he assumed to be the helmsman moving to the adjacent ladder to climb down from the flying bridge. Moments later the last of the Israelis came down the ladder and moved to stand infront of Peter and Michael. It instantly dawned on Peter that this was the man who had beaten him in the fight in George's bar, which was confirmed when the man asked him, "I hope your head is healed and it is not causing you too much pain."

Peter simply glowered in response to the taunt, as the man continued, "I assume it was you who cut the floating packages adrift?"

Peter once again ignored the question and continued to stare into the face of the man, who asked, "You know those packages contained drugs, don't you?"

Peter continued to stare defiantly at the man, who then turned his attention to Michael, saying, "Ah, our little Lebanese friend. I think we have a few questions for you."

Peter pushed himself up to his feet and shouted out as loud as he could, "Just what do you think you bastards are doing."

The Israeli standing by his side, smashed the butt of his Uzi into Peter's unprotected stomach, which made Peter double-up in pain and fall into the corner of the deck, where the heavy wrench was lying, which Peter had eventually adopted as his Plan C.

After a short pause, the leader of the Israelis nodded at one of the men guarding their prisoners, who pulled Michael to his feet and pushed him forward into the cabin of the motor boat. Next the leader of the men turned to the one who had just hit Peter with his weapon and said something in Hebrew to him, but the only bit that Peter understood was that the name 'Uri' had been used, which significantly emphasized to Peter that if they were happy to use their names infront of him, they had no intention of letting him go.

But now Peter was lying on top of a tool that, if it came to a fight, he could use to defend himself. The guard who Peter believed was called Uri, turned and stared at Peter in a manner that showed no hint of mercy, only an evil intent, as the leader of the Israelis and the two other men, one armed with an Uzi sub-machine gun and the other armed with the sawn-off shot gun, accompanied him into the cabin of the motor boat.

Peter, lying in the corner of the deck behind the steps leading down to the cabin, lost sight of the men as they descended the steps, but he concentrated his attention on the man that was guarding him. All he needed was some form of distraction to take the guard's attention off him for a few seconds and he should be able to injure the guard so badly with the wrench, so that he could at least dive in the sea and hopefully swim back to shore.

Peter began to concentrate his thoughts on just how he needed to move, to twist around, get hold of the wrench with his handcuffed hands and bring it down on the head of his guard with sufficient force to incapacitate him for the time he would need to dive over the side of the motor boat into the sea.

As he was working through his options to get hold of the wrench, Peter noted that the conversation he could hear from the cabin of the motor boat had turned to Arabic. Initially, the tone of the questions being asked of Michael was condescending and slightly patronising, but after a few minutes, the tone began to have a menacing edge and soon grew much louder.

Peter only knew a few words of Arabic, so could not understand the vast majority of the questions that soon were being shouted at Michael, which was quickly followed by the distinct sound of a slap.

Michael screamed out in pain and terror, which was soon followed by another slap, that this time sounded much more heavily dealt by his inquisitor. Seconds later Michael's scream was followed by the sound of him crying out Arabic words, which Peter took as a plea of innocence, followed by a flood of wails and tears of distress.

Peter had now rehearsed his actions time and time again in his mind until he was satisfied that given a lapse in his guard's concentration, he could very quickly roll over, take a firm grip on the heavy metal wrench and then crash it down on the head of his Israeli captor. But until that moment came, he was keeping his eyes looking at the floor, just in case Uri read his intentions in his gaze.

More shrieks of torment came from Michael in the cabin of the motor boat, followed by a very heavy thud, which Peter thought sounded like a chair being knocked over violently. This was quickly followed another very loud scream came from the cabin, followed by four rapid incredibly loud shots, which Peter recognized as shot gun blasts.

There was a short few seconds of absolute silence in the cabin, which was just long enough for Uri's eyes to flick over towards the steps that led down to the cabin. Peter could not resist looking in that direction as well and as he looked he saw the head of one of the Israelis, start to come into sight as he slowly stepped backwards up the stairs from the cabin. The man's eyes were looking down in horror at something that was holding his attention in the cabin below.

Unexpectedly there was another incredibly loud shot gun blast that resulted in the Israeli's face being blown to bits, with splatters of blood and flesh splashing out in all directions. The instantly dead body of the Israeli dropped quickly to the deck, just as Peter launched himself into his mentally rehearsed roll, allowing him to get a good grip on the metal wrench and slam it down on Uri's head, with such force that it broke clean through his skull and embedded itself in the soft tissue of his brain.

Even though he knew that he had killed his guard, Peter could not take his eyes off his victim until he heard Michael's voice saying, "And that makes four."

Peter turned and looked at Michael, who had emerged from the cabin of the motor boat, carrying the sawn-off shot gun. He had clearly taken a battering at the hands of his Israeli tormentors, for his face was covered in blood and one of his eyes was already very swollen and bruised.

Peter asked the obvious question, "Are you alright?" To which Michael merely shrugged and said, "Well, at least we are both alive."

Peter was somewhat surprised at how well Michael had stood up to the beating he had received and he also sensed that Michael's answers were a lot more sanguine than he would ever expected to hear from Michael's lips.

In the meantime, Michael helped Peter to his feet and having looked around the deck, he reached down into Uri's pocket and pulled out a key-ring with a small number of keys on it. He carefully checked out the keys until he selected one and came over to Peter and unlocked his handcuffs.

Peter immediately asked, "How did you get free of your handcuffs?" To which Michael replied, "After they slapped me they undid my handcuffs, tied them behind me and sat me on a chair, where I think they planned to beat me in the chest and stomach. But luckily for me, the knot they used to tie my hands was a very weak knot and I easily managed to undo it. When their leader hit me in the chest, I fell over in the chair and managed to grab the shot-gun that the man who tied me up had put down on a table."

Peter nodded to show that he understood how Michael had got free and shoot the Israeli's in the cabin. They next spent a few minutes looking around them at the carnage they had created and as their minds struggled to take it all in, their thoughts started to imagine the consequences of their actions.

Suddenly, a thought struck Peter and he asked, "Why did the men take you down into the cabin and torture you?"

Michael looked at Peter and said, "They wanted to know who had cut free the floating packages of drugs that they intended to smuggle into Cyprus." Michael paused for a moment before carrying on saying, "I think they picked on me just because I am Lebanese and everyone knows that most Israeli's hate Lebanese people.

That seemed to make sense to Peter, who took another look at the bodies in the boat and said, "Well we need to do something with these, otherwise it will take a lot of explaining to the police and I am not sure they will believe our story."

"What shall we do?" Asked Michael.

Peter thought for a minute or two before he moved to the twin-doors that led down to the cabin and picked off a pad-lock that was hanging from its fittings. He held the padlock before Michael and said, "This was clearly designed to secure the doors of the cabin. If we put all the bodies in the cabin and lock them in, along with anything else that might float away and reveal what we have done, we could motor back to near Cape Greco, set the boat on a southerly course, shoot some holes in the bottom of the boat so that it sinks somewhere out there in deep water. We can dive into the sea and swim back to shore and head back to the dive centre as if nothing untoward has happened."

Michael looked Peter in the eyes for a few moments, nodded and said, "That is a good plan." Then he threw the shot gun on to the bench in the cabin, reached down until he could get hold of the feet of the corpse with no face and began to drag him down the steps into the cabin.

Peter did the same with Uri's body. When he got to the bottom of the steps, he looked around the cabin and noticed that two of the Israelis had been shot in the chest, but the leader had also had his face blown off, which Peter thought was a rather worrying thing for an untrained killer like Michael to do, even though he had been mistreated by his tormentors.

Peter moved over to the leader's body and went through his pockets until he found a set of keys, which included one that was fairly clearly the key to the starter of the motor boat. Next he joined Michael in making sure that nothing remained above the deck that could float away and raise interest in the fate of the vessel.

When both of them were satisfied that they had tidied everything away that may incriminate them, Peter closed the twin-doors of the cabin and secured them with the padlock, afterwards he climbed up the ladder to the flying bridge, inserted the ignition key and started the engines of the motor boat.

Before he started up the propellers, Peter spent some minutes looking all around the vessel and scanning the land around the Cape, until he was sure that no one had witnessed their actions or was watching them from the shore. When he was happy that they were unobserved, he set the throttle to forward and steered the boat towards the shoreline where they had started their dive so long ago.

After some ten minutes the boat was about two hundred metres from the shore, so he throttled back the engine until the boat was just slowly coasting along on what little current there was around the Cape. At that moment, the thought suddenly hit him that they had locked all the weapons that the Israelis had in the cabin. He called down to Michael and explained that there was a slight problem with their plan and when he explained that they lacked a weapon to put the holes into the hull of the boat, Michael smiled up to him and moved out of sight beneath the flying bridge for a moment or two, before re-emerging with a smile holding an Uzi. Peter looked at him and said, "I think a burst of machine-gun fire may attract attention. Use the shot gun, which is a more common sound around here. Michael nodded and a few moments later came back with the shot gun. He then went back into the cabin, from where three shot gun blasts echoed up to Peter. Soon afterwards Michael popped back into sight and said, "All is now secure Captain, let's set the ship going and swim back to shore."

Peter went back to the controls, opened up the throttle to move the launch slowly forward, he set the steering wheel so that it was heading roughly south and secured the wheel with some cordage. Finally, he called to Michael to dive into the sea and once he was safely swimming back towards the shore, Peter opened up the throttle of the launch and afterwards he also dived into the sea and soon caught up with Michael.

After a few minutes they stopped swimming and turned to watch the launch head steadily southwards. Soon they could see that it was slowly beginning to sink lower into the water. By the time they had reached the shore, the launch was at least one mile out to sea and clearly sinking lower and lower into the water, until the engine coughed several times, then spluttered to silence and a few minutes later, the launch sunk beneath the waves. Peter remarked, "At that distance off-shore, it must now lie in well over 100 metres of water, which makes it incredibly unlikely that divers will ever reach it and I can't see that a vessel with high definition sonar will ever go to the trouble of investigating it, even if one happens to spot it on its sonar."

Michael nodded in response and as Peter was looking at Michael he noted that although they had both been swimming for some time, Michael still had some blood marks on his face and neck. Peter explained what the problem was and washed away the traces of blood, before they climbed back up the rocks from the Canyon and picking up there previously abandoned diving equipment, they loaded it on to their truck.

When the loading was complete, they both looked at each other for some time, until Peter said to Michael, "We must be clear with each other. All we have done this morning is enjoy a good dive from Canyon, during which the only things we saw were some nice Roughback rays."

Michael nodded saying, "I agree. And don't forget, I will be flying back to Beirut on Saturday, so you don't have to worry about me going to the police."

Peter nodded in agreement, then turned and the two of them climbed into the cab of the truck and after a few minutes they began their drive back to the dive centre.

+ + + + +

As soon as they got back to the dive centre, Michael packed his things into the boot of his Nissan and turned to Peter and thanked him for the dives they had done over the last week or so. As they shook hands he simply said, "I will remember this week for many years and if I ever come back to Cyprus, I will telephone you and hopefully we can do some more diving." Then he opened the door of his car, sat inside it and started the engine, closed the door and with a wave of his hand he drove off up the hill back into Ayia Napa.

After Peter had returned the wave, he turned and went up the steps into the dive centre, where he found Elena sitting behind the counter, rearranging the flowers that Michael had left for her in the tall blue glass flower bowl she kept under the counter for such occasions. Peter told her that Michael had bought the flowers and that he had been in a bit of a hurry, so he had driven off as soon as he could when they got back from their dive at the Canyon.

Elena replied that she would have liked to have thanked Michael for the flowers and said goodbye to him as she doubted that they would ever see him again. Peter told her that Michael had thanked him for the dives they had done and also mentioned that Michael had indicated that he would like to do some more dives with them, if he ever came back to Cyprus. But Elena stopped him by saying that she always felt there was something a little strange in the man and she for one wouldn't be too upset if they never saw him again. She followed on by asking how the dive at Canyon had been and Peter did his very best to make his report sound like it had just been another typical dive at Canyon, where they had enjoyed the company of a good number of Roughback Stingrays. When he had finished his report he looked into Elena's eyes and noted that she had one of her strange looks on her face. She pondered his response for a moment or two and said, "You had better tell me what is troubling you, for I can see it in your face and hear it in your words."

Peter gave a little shrug with his shoulders and told her that she was being silly. The dive had been fine and nothing untoward had happened.

Elena finally smiled at him and said, "So Michael paid you for the dive I assume."

Peter was totally lost for words. In the emotion of the events he had completely forgotten about taking his payment from Michael, who had now left them for the last time, without paying for his final dive. All he could do was apologise to Elena saying, "I'm sorry darling, I completely forgot to take his money and now he had gone back to Larnaca and I don't even know where he has been staying.

Elena, raised her head and said, "But I know his telephone number. I have written it in the booking book and you can give him a call and remind him that he still owes us for the dive." To which Peter grinned at her and said that he was lucky to have the cleverest wife on the island and he would give Michael a call straightaway. But only a few seconds later he realized that

Michael would still be on his way back to Larnaca, so they would have to wait for a while before telephoning him.

Later that afternoon, Peter did make a call to the number Elena had written in the office diary for Michael, but the constant tone he got from the other end indicated that the line was now dead. All he could do was tell Elena that it looked as if Michael had already ended his contract with CYTA, the Cypriot telephone company, and it was, therefore, impossible to contact him again.

Elena gave him another one of her looks, this time the one that indicated that she thought her husband was a little bit retarded, and admonished him by saying, "Well, make sure that it doesn't happen again. We rely on the money we make from diving to pay for the things we like."

Later that afternoon they closed up the dive centre and went down to George's restaurant where Elena helped her father out with the cooking for a few hours before they all headed back to their homes in Vrysoules. When they reached the village, Elena walked George back home and made sure he was going to be alright for the night, then she walked back to where Peter was waiting for her in the garden and they finally closed the door and got ready for another night of disturbed sleep.

Chapter 11
Thursday, 20th August 1987

On this day, when they opened up the dive centre, Elena reminded Peter that he had arranged to visit a hotel near Pernera beach which was managed by a Mr. Perdios, where they had been informed that there were some potential novice divers who were keen to have a trial experience in the hotel's swimming pool, prior to booking a Novice Trial Dive. She also reminded him that after he returned from that event, Father Loucas was coming over to see them in George's restaurant to have a quick chat about Maroulla's funeral.

It didn't take Peter long to load up the truck with enough diving equipment for the trial dive in the swimming pool. So, after he had told Elena that he was heading off, he got into his truck and started the drive back over the Cape Greco road. As he dropped off the headland of Cape Greco, he drove past the sign that pointed to Fig Tree Bay and eventually turned right off the main road, on to a track that eventually led to the hotel by Pernera beach.

He parked his truck by the side of the hotel, where it would be easy for him to carry his diving equipment to the swimming pool and walked around to the hotel's reception, where he greeted Andrea, a lovely young lady who also lived in Vrysoules village and had worked at the hotel for some years. He liked to keep a good relationship with her, because she always recommended the services of Peter and Elena to any potential diving customers.

So, after complimenting Andrea on the dress she was wearing, Peter pointed out to her that they had been informed that there were two guests at the hotel who had requested that they try a test dive in the swimming pool. Andrea asked if he knew their names and he replied by saying that he only knew that they had booked dives in the name of Mr. Ryan Pinney. Andrea quickly checked through the reception's notes and after a nod of confirmation she said that the guest's names were Miss Taylor Whiteman and Mr. Ryan Pinney, two British guests who had been at the hotel for a few days and were keen to experience a dive in the clear waters of the Mediterranean Sea.

She then rang their room, but got no answer, so she asked one of the bell boys to go around the swimming pool, calling out the names of the two guests and when he found them he was instructed to tell them that the scuba diving instructor had arrived and would soon be setting up his equipment at the shallow end of the hotel's swimming pool.

Ten minutes later, as Peter was testing the regulator of the scuba set, a young couple approached him and introduced themselves as Taylor and Ryan. Both of them were British tourists, who had noted in their holiday guides that there was an opportunity to do a trial dive at the hotel and both stressed just how much they were looking forward to the experience. Peter assured them that the swimming pool trial would be free, but if they were happy breathing off a cylinder in the swimming pool, he would gladly take them for a novice dive in the sea for thirty-five Cypriot pounds per person. They both readily agreed to this proposal and so Peter asked them who would like to go first. Ryan nobly suggested that it was always polite to let the lady go first, so Taylor found herself being lowered into the swimming pool and the scuba set was secured on her back. Peter gave both of them a short briefing on what was going to happen and stated that the dive would be perfectly safe as long as the diver breathed in and out continuously and never held their breath.

After he had shown Taylor how to spit in her face mask to stop it misting up, which she very self-consciously did with the very minimum of saliva, she finally followed Peter's instruction to drop down on to her knees so that her head was just below the surface and simply practise breathing off the cylinder. When she had mastered this skill, Peter pulled her back to her feet and said that he would now guide her around the pool so she could experience the sensation of diving underwater. Peter helped her back on to her knees again and using the pillar valve of the cylinder as a handle, he gently guided her around the pool for some minutes, before he helped her stand up again, at the place where she had started her adventure. Taylor was so pleased with the experience that she instantly dispelled any worries Ryan had about the exercise and soon he was being led around the pool by Peter. After Ryan came back to the surface with a big smile on his face, Peter was pretty sure that they would sign up for the Novice Dive in Green Bay, so he helped Ryan take of the diving gear and sure enough both of them gushed with enthusiasm to go on the Novice Dive. He advised them that he could take them for a dive in Green Bay on Saturday morning and he would pick them up from the hotel's reception at nice o'clock in the morning. All they needed to bring along was their swim wear and their wallets and he promised them an experience they would never forget. After he had thanked them for their business, Peter packed up the diving equipment and loaded it back on the truck and after checking that all was secure, he headed back to Ayia Napa.

On the drive back his thoughts suddenly returned to the awful events of yesterday. Strangely he had slept very soundly through the night, which he hadn't expected, even though he was aware from his Army life that stress drains a lot of energy from the body. This often has the affect of making soldiers who have had a bad day on operations feel very tired at the end of their patrol.

His thoughts turned again to the chances of the boat with its bodies being discovered, but when he added up the risks of that happening balanced against the depth and remoteness of the place where they now lay on the seabed, he returned to the conclusion that there was really very little chance of the launch being discovered and retrieved.

When he got back to the dive centre, he unloaded the diving gear and gave it a good wash, since swimming pool water can often be more corrosive to diving gear than sea water. Just as he was folding away the hose pipe, Elena came to join him and reminded him that they had an appointment with Father Loucas in George's restaurant.

So, they locked up the dive centre, leaving a sign on the door that if anyone wanted them they could be found in the nearby Harbour Restaurant, then they walked down to the restaurant where they found George, serving a few customers with drinks and food. They quickly found a table near the bar and sat down waiting for George to come over and offer them some lunch and a refreshing drink of Cypriot cola.

Just a little over an hour later, Father Loucas appeared in the door of the restaurant and once his eyes got used to the lower light in the place, he waved to Peter and Elena and came across to join them at their table. George soon came over to ask what the priest would like to eat and drink, to which he simply asked for a Cyprus coffee served with lots of sugar, or 'Glykos Kafes' in the soft Greek language.

The three of them made small talk, until George brought the coffee across to their table, with its traditional glass of cold water. Moments later the mood quickly changed to a more sombre tone as Father Loucas briefed them on what arrangements he had made for the funeral of Maroulla. He started by telling them that due to the police investigation, Maroulla would remain in the mortuary of Larnaca hospital for at least another week or two. Next he stated that he had checked with the local government and church authorities and everyone agreed that as soon as Maroulla was returned her funeral would take place in the church of Ayios Demitrios in Frenaros village.

The church in Frenaros was the nearest church to Vrysoules village and Maroulla's father and mother were buried in the same place as she would be interred. Finally he told them a few more details that he had arranged, before ending the briefing which he could see was causing George a lot of distress.

To lighten the air a little, Father Loucas turned to Peter and said, "I hear you have been asking questions about the church of Ayioi Anargiroi?"

Peter could not remember asking any questions about the church above Chapel Cave, but as his curiosity was still running high after Michael's discovery of the ring, he was quite happy for the priest to continue on the subject. So he replied that he was interested to learn about the history of the Ayioi Anargiroi Church.

Father Loucas relaxed back into his chair and started with, "It is a church that has fascinated me for a long time. Why is it there? Why such a remote location? Well Peter, I am afraid I have very little hard facts to tell you about the church, but I have a lot of legends about the place.

The first legend, or possibly a fact, is that the cave beneath the church has been a home to quite a few hermits over the centuries and one body of priests believe that this is the reason for the church being built there. They would simply live in the cave, staring out to sea. No one really knows why they would do it, but they would sometimes spend years in the cave, with just that one view of the world. They are often referred to a members of the Stoicism movement. Some scholars believed that the hermits could clear their minds of worldly concerns and concentrate on more deeper religious thoughts.

However, I believe a far older legend. There are references in some very old church records that tell that the church was built on the site of an ancient Greek goddess called Aphrodite. She was the most popular Greek god in Cyprus in pre-Christian times. She was the goddess of love and the sea, for the story goes that she was born out of the foam at the place we now call Petra tou Romiou, which is near Paphos and the Tourist Board refer to it as Aphrodite's Rock. Obviously, with the coming of Christianity to Cyprus, many old temples to the Greek gods were used to build the new Christian Churches. It was a way of burying the old gods and establishing the new God.

But there is also older stories, that even before the temple to Aphrodite was built, there was a far older religious use of the site. If you think of the bay that lies infront of the church, it is a very safe place to anchor a ship in bad weather, especially if the wind is blowing in from the west. Therefore, one story tells that the site was first used as the location for a Pharos, or Warning Fire, a Beacon. This was the origin of today's lighthouse. The Pharos would have been lit when a storm was building up to guide prehistoric wooden trading ships towards a safe haven from the storm. The earliest ships that would have been used for trade in those times would have been Phoenician vessels, which we know used a trade route from Byblos, Sidon and Tyre, to carry cargoes for trade with other countries, including Egypt, Carthage and ancient Cyprus. It just makes sense to have a

Pharos standing high above the sea, which would have been visible for many miles to the east, where Phoenicia lay and the headland of Cape Greco is precisely such a place.

The tale then goes on to say, that because there was a Pharos on the site for many years, eventually the Pharos was dedicated to the Phoenician god of fire and War, the evil god we now refer to as Baal. He was also known by the attractive title of 'First and Principal King of Hell'."

At this point, Peter could not resist mentioning the ring that Michael had found, so he interrupted the priest's story by telling him, "I was diving just outside the cave below Ayioi Anargiroi Church, when a visiting diver from the Lebanon, found a huge gold ring with a motif of flames on its face. Do you think that the ring could have anything to do with Baal?"

Father Loucas thought for a moment before he replied, "No, I don't think so Peter. I am talking about events that occurred three thousand years ago and I don't think a ring would last that long in the sea. Surely it would simply be eaten away by the salt water, or it would be covered in marine concretion over all those years."

Peter responded by telling the priest that gold has amazing properties, that include the fact that it never rots away in salt water and for some scientific reason, gold rarely is affected by concretion.

Father Loucas next asked the obvious question, "What happened to the ring?"

Peter assured him that he had given clear instructions to the visiting diver that he must hand the ring in to the Department of Antiquities and the diver had told him that he had indeed handed the ring in to the authorities in Larnaca. He also added that the ring was the biggest gold ring he had ever seen and just had to be worth a fortune, even if it was just for the amount of gold it contained.

Father Loucas nodded his head and said, "That is the right thing to do and if I had known about it I would certainly have backed-up the handing in of the ring, for if it did have anything at all to do with Baal, I would get rid of it as quickly as possible. You never know what evil there may be in the ring."

After a few moments pause for effect, he continued, "Anyhow, the story goes that the site of the Pharos later became associated with Baal, until the Greek gods came to prominence in Cyprus and the site was used to build the temple to Aphrodite on, just as later the Christian Church was built over the remains of the temple to Aphrodite."

At that moment, George interrupted the conversation to ask if they wanted any more drinks, so Peter was left to ponder on all that Father Loucas had told him. It just fitted in so well with the flames motif on the ring and the obvious fact that it was so big and heavy, it must have had some ceremonial usage.

He was still deep in thought about the ring when he noticed that Elena was standing by her father with his keys held up infront of George's face as a subtle hint that it was time to close up the restaurant and make the journey home.

George responded by thanking Father Loucas for all he had done and informing everyone in the restaurant that they would have to drink up as he would be closing the place in ten minutes time. Father Loucas spoke gently to George to remind him that if he needed any help at all, the church was always there to come to his assistance. Finally, he turned to Peter and said that if he ever had any more questions about the church of Ayioi Anargiroi, or any other church, he would be delighted to do all he could to help. Finally, Father Loucas bid everyone "Kali Spera", and nodding to everyone he passed he left the restaurant.

Eventually, when everyone had left and George had tidied up the place and finally locked the doors, they drove back to their homes in Vrysoules.

Soon after they returned home Peter turned on the radio tuned to the British Forces radio station, to catch up with news from Cyprus and the UK. The news from England was full of a dreadful shooting incident in the town of Hungerford. The report stated that during the previous day a strange loner called Michael Ryan had gone on a shooting spree around the town of Hungerford, which was in the south of England and had shot sixteen people. The tally included a police constable and Michael Ryan's mother. The gunman had been armed with an assortment of fire arms. The shooting had lasted for several hours before it finally ended when he took his own life.

Both Peter and Elena listened to the grim news for some time before Elena turned to Peter, with tears in her eyes and sobbed the words, "Why is the world so awful?"

Chapter 12
Friday, 21st August 1987

The day started very hot indeed. There was not a cloud in the sky as Peter and Elena parked the truck outside the dive centre. Elena unlocked the dive centre and after checking with the diary, confirmed to Peter that the only booking he had that day was for an old English diver, called William. This very experienced diver had been the Diving Officer of the British Army's diving centre in Dhekelia many years earlier. William was staying on holiday with his wife at the Tsokkos Brothers hotel in Fig Tree Bay. Peter had dived with this old friend many times over the years and always looked forward to each dive they did together. William invariably had funny or informative tales to tell of his diving days in the late 1960s, when diving was far less technical than it later became. But as the dive was not booked until two o'clock in the afternoon, they would have some time to check over the state of the diving equipment, especially the wet suits, to make sure that all was in good order. Later, he loaded up enough diving equipment for the afternoon's dive with William, which was made easier because he knew precisely which size of wet suit would fit his customer and what type of face mask and regulator he preferred.

At eleven o'clock they both went over to George's restaurant. Elena had volunteered to once again help her father with the cooking, so she gave him a peck on the cheek as she walked into the kitchen area, lifting an apron off the back of the door as she went.

Peter pulled out a bar stool from underneath the bar and sat near to where George was washing a few of the less frequently used glasses. He asked how George had slept and received the expected reply, "Etsi Ketsi", which was the common Greek phrase for 'so so'. Moments later George looked up from washing the glasses and Peter noticed just how old he was now looking. George asked Peter if he would like a coffee or something else. Peter felt so sorry for his beloved father-in-law, who had really taken on the role of a father in Peter's mind. Peter had never known a father-figure in his childhood, but had formed his own impression of how a father should look and behave from television programmes and films. Then he had been lucky enough to meet a wonderful young Cypriot lady, who had such wonderful parents and he had slowly come to appreciate all the little things that make a good father and mother. His heart was breaking as he watched George try to tackle his grief, which was clearly physically weakening the man he idolized.

Forcing himself to think, Peter ordered a Cyprus Nescafe coffee and when George served it to him he sipped at it slowly, as he tried to make small talk about anything that would keep George from thinking sad thoughts.

Peter asked his father-in-law if anyone had heard anything more of the four Israeli men who had caused the fight in his restaurant and George answered that he hadn't heard any reference to those bullies since he had contacted the police to report the incident which had led to Peter being attacked by the men. He followed this up by saying that he thought they must be long gone from Cyprus. Probably because they knew they were in trouble with the authorities and didn't want to risk being arrested. This was just what Peter was hoping he would hear, so he tried to lift the mood a little by making light of it by adding, "They should think themselves lucky that they caught me on a bad day. Normally I would have smashed all their faces in, but I couldn't find my tin of Spinach."

Peter was very pleased to see that his little joke had cheered George up enough to produce a little smile on his face. He looked over the bar to Peter and said, "Perhaps a bowl of Tahini would have given you even more strength."

Peter agreed and they kept up a light banter between themselves until Peter noted that the clock above the bar was telling him that it was approaching half past one, so he made his apologies to George, saying he had a dive booking at two o'clock. After he stood up from his chair, he stuck his head around the door of the kitchen and shouted across to Elena that he was off now to pick up the dive booking and he should be back by around five o'clock. Elena nodded to him and told him to be careful and enjoy the dive, before she turned back to the kitchen range and continued to work on the food orders for the restaurant's clients. Peter walked back to his truck, which sat fully loaded in the parking space behind the dive centre, climbed into the driver's seat and started the drive across to Fig Tree Bay.

+ + + + +

When he arrived at Fig Tree Bay, William was waiting with his wife in the reception of the hotel. Peter spotted him immediately he entered the hotel and greeted him warmly as a respected fellow diver. Peter was well aware that William had more or less the same diving qualifications as he had, but William had dived in many more places and countries than Peter could ever hope to compete with. Not only that, but William always managed to teach Peter something new, whenever they had dived together in the past, so naturally, Peter was really looking forward to another dive with his old friend.

"Where do you fancy diving today?" Asked Peter.

"Do you know Cow's Cave?" Replied William.

"No." Replied Peter, "But I am always keen to learn of new dive sites."

"It is on the northern point of the bay in which Chapel Cave sits." Said William.

"Oh, I know the place, but I didn't know it was called Cow's Cave." Stated Peter, "Do you know why it is called Cow's Cave?"

"Someone told me once that a local farmer used to house his cow in the cave. But I don't know how true that is. All I know is that it drops off very quickly from the headland there, but if you go due south from the cave, there are some really nice reefs that aren't too deep to fin over. So I think it should be okay for me, as I haven't dived deep since the last time I dived with you last year."

Peter agreed and after William had kissed his wife and assured her that he would be careful, they turned to leave the hotel, but just as they headed for the doors of the hotel, Peter spotted the manager of the hotel, Mr. Perdios, leaving his office by the reception. So, after asking William if it was okay to have a chat with Mr. Perdios, Peter called out his name and went over to greet him by shaking his hand.

Peter had a lot of respect for Mr. Perdios, who was a very popular manager, both with his staff and his clients. He always seemed to be aware of everything that was going on in his hotel and was always open to suggestions and positive criticism from his team and guests. He was also a great supporter of Peter and Elena's dive centre and would always recommend them to anyone who made any enquiries about diving while staying in his hotel.

When he had finished shaking Mr. Perdios' hand, Peter introduced him to William and strongly sang the praises of Mr. Perdios to his old diving friend. Mr. Perdios asked where they were going to dive and Peter explained that they were going to the northern headland of the bay above Cape Greco, Mr. Perdios said, "Oh, you mean Cyclops' Cave."

Peter was silly enough to tell the hotel manager that he had been informed that it was called Cow's Cave and then followed it up by asking why he thought it was called Cyclops' Cave.

Mr. Perdios answered with a twinkle in his eye, that it was called Cyclops' Cave, because Cyclops used to live there.

Peter responded with, "I really shouldn't have asked that, should I?" To which both Mr. Perdios and William nodded their heads, before the hotel manager told them that he wouldn't keep them talking any longer as they had a dive to do and bid them, "Kalo Taxidi."

After responding to Mr. Perdios with a cheerful "Adieu." Peter led William to his truck and they both began the drive down to "Whatever the cave was called".

+ + + + +

Fifteen minutes later Peter stopped his truck at the end of yet another challenging Cyprus track. The track ended where the sandy soil changed to hard black rocky stretches with very sharp points liberally scattered about, that would easily rip the tyres of the truck to shreds. They both climbed out of the truck and began to change into their diving wet suits and equipment.

As they were getting changed Peter happened to look down the coast and saw that there was a fairly large truck parked alongside the burned out ruin of the Ayioi Anargiroi Church. He tapped his old friend on the arm and said, "Have you heard that the church above Chapel Cave burned down a few days ago?"

William responded that he had heard the bad news and went on to say that he really liked that old church. As he turned his head to look at the church and after squinting for a minute or two, he said, "Isn't there a truck up there, loading something off by the church?"

Peter responded by saying, "Yes. It certainly looks as if something is being unloaded up there. Perhaps they are going to start the restoration of the church straightaway. But I can't make out what it is that they are unloading up there. Can you?"

William gave him a wry smile and said, "Not with these old eyes I'm afraid."

Peter suddenly remembered that he had a small pair of binoculars in the glove compartment of his truck, so he took them out of their case and focused them on the truck. After peering at the scene for some minutes, he pulled the binos down from his eyes, saying, "No. I can't really see what they are unloading. Whatever it is seems to be long rods or wooden beams, or something like that, so perhaps they are planning on rebuilding the church."

Turning to William he said, "Well, let's forget about that for a moment and concentrate on making sure you enjoy your dive."

When they were both fully kitted out in their wet suits and diving gear, they gingerly found their way from the end of the track to the cave and eventually down to the water's edge, where Peter led the way into the sea. As they entered the water, it was only waist deep, so they found it easy to fit on their fins, their masks and with their regulators securely held in their right hands, they waded out into deeper water.

Once both the divers were sorted out, they exchanged 'OK' hand signals and both of them emptied all the air out of their buoyancy compensators, before they kicked their legs in the air to get underwater and start their dive.

Initially, they finned south over a sandy bottom until, after a few moments they were finning over a large field of eel grass. As the eel grass gave way to yet another stretch of sand, they began to see the common sea creatures of Cyprus. The first one seen was a long black sea cucumber which at first glance looked like a discarded section of corrugated rubber hose. Only its mouth with moving small tentacles indicated that it was a living sea creature. Next they encountered a dispersed shoal of Damsel fish, with a few Red Squirrel fish for company.

Peter suddenly felt a tap on his arm and when he looked at William, he saw that his old friend was indicating that they should turn about forty-five degrees to their right and head in a more southerly-westerly direction. Peter nodded to show that he understood and they both began finning in the direction indicated by William.

Gradually the sandy bottom began to drop away into deeper water and after a few minutes more of finning, Peter began to see that they were heading towards some large rocky reefs. As he peered into the slightly gloomy water ahead of them, darkened by the absorption of reds and yellows in the deepening water, he noticed that there were one or two decent sized Groupers leisurely swimming around the rocky reefs. They continued to swim towards the fish until the Groupers grew unhappy about the approaching divers and headed into gaps in the rocks. These were the first decent sized Groupers that Peter had seen for some time, so he pulled his Nikonos 4 camera from the thigh pocket of his wet suit and tried to take some photos of them, but without success as whenever he got close to a Grouper, it immediately shot off into a rock crevice.

Growing frustrated, Peter turned to look at William, with the aim of taking a few photos of his friend, but soon decided against this action as at the depth they were now finning the light had faded so much that only blues and greens remained of the light spectrum.

He did, however, notice that William was up to his old habits of testing sponges to see if they were the right type to make into bath sponges. William noticed that he was attracting the attention of Peter and gave an emphasized shrug of his shoulders, that indicated to Peter that William realized that he had been caught out once again getting up to his old tricks, but it really didn't bother the old rogue too much.

Eventually, William reached back and caught hold of his pressure gauge, which he inspected and afterwards held it up to Peter for his information. Peter noted that William's air pressure was down to just a fraction over one hundred bars, so he gave an 'OK' signal to show that he acknowledged the pressure gauge reading and pointed back up the slope, towards where they had entered the water. William simply nodded and began to gracefully turn back up the slope.

Ten minutes later their heads broke through the surface of the water, just metres from where they had entered the sea. Peter took his regulator out of his mouth and said to William, "Was that okay for you?" To which William simply nodded and taking out his own regulator he said, "Just as good as I remembered it from the old days. Besides, the fact that there are now only small groupers swimming around. In the nineteen seventies, you were sometimes lucky enough to see five feet long groupers, and they were really a wonderful site. There was one that lived on the Ormidhia Wreck that was at least five feet in length and often came out to meet divers. Interestingly, we discovered that it liked to eat Roast Chicken flavoured crisps."

Peter shook his head and replied as he waded into shallower water to take his fins off, "You always have a nice story to tell William. I don't suppose you remember its name?"

William, who by that time was also in shallow water, pulling off his fins replied without looking up, "We called it George, but that was just our name, for he never really introduced himself." Peter gave a little laugh as he helped William out of the sea and up the little climb to the top of the small rocky cliff and they started back across the sharp rocks towards the truck.

After another ten minutes, they had both de-kitted and loaded their equipment on to the truck and dried themselves with their towels, before they changed back into their T-shirts and shorts.

At this point, William reached into the foot well on the passenger's side of the truck and pulled a Thermos flask out of his shoulder bag. He poured a mug full of iced orange juice out of the Thermos and offered first sip to Peter. Peter thanked him, drank half the contents of the mug and handed it back to William, with a few words of thanks. William drank the other half of the mug, before shaking it over the sandy soil to get rid of the last droplets in the mug, before he screwed it back on to the top of the Thermos flask.

After a short while William turned and looked back towards the church above Chapel Cave and said, "You know there was one odd thing that sticks out in my memory about that old church. My wife claims that she is a bit of a psychic medium and whenever she approached the church, she always claimed that she could sense some form of malign presence. Even our dog that we had at the time, would always whine whenever it got too near the place. I don't personally believe in all that mumbo-jumbo, but when I mentioned to her that I fancied diving at Cow's Cave, the first thing she said was that I wasn't to venture too near to the church." Peter didn't mention the church above Chapel Cave again on the way back to William's hotel, but he did have a lot to think about on his drive back to the dive centre in Ayia Napa.

+ + + + +

By the time Peter drove back to his normal parking space behind the dive centre he was in a bit of a quandary. He had been thinking about William remarks concerning the Ayioi Anargiroi Church and he didn't know whether to tell Elena what William had told him. Therefore, when he found that she wasn't in the dive centre he was a little relieved that she had solved the dilemma for him.

He decided he would unload the truck and wash all the diving gear they had used for their dive, before going to see Elena in George's restaurant, where she would no doubt be helping her father deal with the day's trade.

As he was washing the equipment and the wet suits he noticed that the one William had been wearing had developed a little bit of damage along the stitching of one arm, so after he had washed it he carefully repaired the stitching with his own noble efforts.

After he had checked that everything was back in good order and replaced in the right locations, he decided it was time to go and report in to Elena, so he locked up the dive centre and walked across to George's bar.

As he entered the bar he found George working away as normal, chatting with his customers and serving them with their drinks. Peter decided he would have a quick chat with his father-in-law, just to see how he was feeling, before he went into the kitchen to see Elena.

George greeted Peter and asked him what he would like to drink, to which Peter responded by requesting a glass of fresh orange juice with some ice, as although it was now just after five o'clock in the afternoon, the temperature outside was still well above thirty degrees centigrade. George nodded at the order and went to the back of the bar where he kept his orange juice extractor, into which he placed the first of the oranges that he would crush to extract the juice. As he was doing this Peter asked him how trade had been that day, to which George replied that it had been really busy earlier with lots of orders for food. Peter replied, "Well, at least that would have given Elena something to keep her busy."

George looked at him and said over his shoulder, "But Elena left the kitchen at about three o'clock this afternoon. Luckily for me, Alexandros' mother, Yolande, was able to stand in for her and she has really worked hard all afternoon. So I am very grateful to her."

He said this as he turned to Peter and placed his glass of chilled orange juice on the bar infront of him.

Peter stared at George in a perplexed manner for some seconds, before he said, "Do you know why she left at three o'clock?"

George looked at him and said, "No. All she said was that wanted to check on something in the booking diary, then she took off her apron and went back to the dive centre and I haven't seen anything of her since then."

Peter took a quick long drink of the orange juice and told George that he would just pop back over to the dive centre and see if Elena had left any notes or clues as to where she had gone. By this time, George was looking just as anxious as Peter was, so as Peter walked towards the door of the restaurant, he shouted across to him, "Please come straight back and tell me that everything is alright, so that I don't worry."

Peter raised his hand in acknowledgement and strode as quickly as he could to the dive centre. When he entered the building he went straight to the bookings diary and checked to see if she had written something in there that would explain her absence, but the only entry on the page marked, 'August 21st' was the single booking for William at '14:00 hours'. Peter looked around the office for any other clues that would indicate where Elena had gone, but with no success. In frustration, he searched below the counter and all through the working area and kitchen at the back of the dive centre, but once again there was nothing to explain the mystery of her disappearance.

Eventually, Peter gave up the search and quickly walked back to George's bar. George instantly looked up at him as he entered the doors and asked if he knew where Elena had gone. Peter shook his head and said, "Not a clue. I just hope nothing has happened to her."

George, in the meantime, had virtually collapsed into a chair near the bar and suddenly Peter began to realise just how much George had suffered from the death of his wife and now with the disappearance of his adored daughter, the darkest of thoughts were surging through his mind. At that moment, George's head jerked up and turning to Peter with tears in his eyes, he asked if Peter had rung home, for Elena might be there.

Peter replied that he hadn't rung home because he didn't understand how Elena could have got back to Vrysoules, when he had the truck. But seeing how much distress this answer was causing George, Peter smiled and said, "But if I may use your telephone, I will ring home now."

Peter walked behind the bar to where George kept the telephone and rang their home number. As he held the telephone to his ear, listening to the repeated ringing sounds, he prayed fervently in his mind for Elena to answer the phone, so that he could hear her beautiful voice reassure him that all was well, but no reply came to his phone call. When the telephone had rung for some minutes, he looked at George and shook his head as he reluctantly returned the telephone to its cradle and said to George, "No reply."

By now, George was becoming obviously distraught at the situation and after thinking for a few moments, he stood up and walked to the door of the kitchen, shouting in Greek, to ask Yolande if she would mind the bar while he drove back to Vrysoules to find Elena. Yolande turned and asked in a worried voice, why George needed to check on Elena, to which George briefly replied by telling her that he was worried about his daughter. Yolande quickly informed him that she would indeed look after the bar in his absence and also told them to get home as quickly as they could and ring her to tell her that everything had been sorted out.

With no more prompting, George and Peter left the bar, walked over to Peter's truck and headed out of the village on to the road to Vrysoules.

+ + + + +

By the time they reached Vrysoules it was half past six in the evening. As soon as Peter had pulled up outside their home, he and George rammed open the doors of the truck and rushed up to the house as quickly as they could. As they ran, both Peter and George were calling out the name "Elena", and when they reached the door of the house, they burst through the door, which as normal had been left unlocked, as they continued loudly calling out her name. But to no response.

Peter and George looked at each other and George said he would go to his house and check if Elena was there. He added that she might have gone there to do some laundry for him, which would have meant that she may not have heard the telephone ringing.

Peter nodded and said that he would check out the garden and if he did not find her there he would walk over to the supermarket in case she had gone shopping. But in his mind he was still deeply worried because he could not figure out how she could have got home without the truck.

However, before Peter had looked in every possible place in the garden, George had returned from his house to let Peter know that there was no sign of Elena at his home. Both men looked at each other and each could see the distress that the other was going through in their search for Elena. George shook his head as a sign of despair and suggested that they walk down on to the main road in the village and see is she was in the supermarket.

By seven o'clock, they had reached the supermarket and while Peter searched up and down the aisles, George asked the daughter of the owner, if she had seen Elena at all that day. When both of them came to the conclusion that Elena had not been in the supermarket during the day, they met up at the tills and with shoulders slumped they walked out of the store and stood in desolation, just outside shop.

Both of them were now racking their brains to think of a simple and safe solution to Elena's disappearance, but without saying the words they dreaded to say to the other, both of them now had horrible premonitions of just what had happened to her.

As they walked back to Peter's house for a final check to see if she was safely home, they both agreed that if she wasn't there, they should inform the police of her disappearance. Peter tried to be upbeat about calling the police, saying, "At least we know that calling the police is the right thing to do, even if we both get our ears burned when she suddenly turns up safe and sound and scolds us for wasting the police's time."

It took them a little more than ten minutes to get back to their houses and when they reached the gate of Peter's house they stopped and ran over their plans again. Peter was going to ring the dive centre one more time to see if Elena was there, which he very much doubted as he had locked the dive centre up and had brought the keys home with him, but there was the off-chance that Elena had found the place locked up and was waiting for him to come and pick her up. In the meantime, George would ring Yolande in the restaurant and see if Elena had shown up there. George would telephone the police and report her disappearance and afterwards wait at home in case she suddenly turned up at either of their houses.

If Peter did not get a positive response to his telephone call, he would drive once more down to the dive centre and see is she was waiting there for him and if she wasn't there he would check the local area and see if anyone had any sightings of her. He would obviously keep making telephone calls to George, to keep both of them in touch with any news that they learned.

Both men nodded at each other and turned to walk into their homes. Peter immediately picked up the telephone and rang the dive centre. When there was no answer, he let the telephone ring for another twenty-five times, before he put it down and picked it up again straightaway. This time he rang George's house, but initially he only got the engaged tone, for George was still in conversation with either Yolande at the restaurant, or the police to report Elena's disappearance. After a further two or three attempts, George picked up the phone and answered. When he found it was Peter, he told him that he had checked with Yolande and there was still no sign of Elena, so he had reported the issue to the police, who had told him that they would be sending someone over to interview him from their Paralimni office. Peter followed on by telling him that he would set off in a minute or so for the dive centre and if he didn't find her there, he would make his own enquiries with the local businesses around the dive centre. When he hung up the telephone, he checked that he had the car keys and the keys for the dive centre in his pockets before he walked out to his truck and set off for the drive back down to Ayia Napa.

By the time he reached the village of Dheryneia it was just past seven thirty in the evening and he noticed that the sun was beginning to go down over the Troodos Mountains to the west of Cyprus. As he had been driving, his mind had been going through all the possibilities that could have caused Elena to have disappeared. So much had happened in the last few days that could have been linked with someone kidnapping her or doing her serious harm. He simply would not let his mind consider that she may have met a similar fate to Maroulla, but he found it a struggle to dismiss this appalling outcome.

There was also something else that was troubling his mind and that was the burning down of the Ayioi Anargiroi Church, plus what William and he had seen at the remains of the church and William's comments about the evil presence his wife was reported to have felt whenever she got too near to it. Could all this be somehow linked to Elena's disappearance?

Eventually, Peter took the snap decision that as he would be driving along the road past Cape Greco, he would divert and visit the ruins of the church above Chapel Cave, just to set his mind at rest. Therefore, he put his foot down a little harder on to the accelerator until the truck began to bounce a little too much for his comfort, but when he reached the junction by Cape Greco, he turned left and after the short drive to the turn off to Chapel Cave, he slowed down so as to limit the amount of noise his trusty old truck made and started the drive down to the ruins of the church.

A few minutes later, he went past the natural rock arch that some people referred to as the Lovers' Bridge, which was just north of the ruins of the church and more or less in sight of the headland on which the church had been built. At this point, he switched off his headlights, so that he wouldn't make his approach to obvious in the failing light of the evening. The moon was already visible, but it was only a sliver of light for it was approaching the date of the New Moon. He drove for another fifty metres, then gently brought the truck to a halt. After he had quietly opened the glove compartment of his truck and taken out his reliable underwater torch, he cautiously opened the driver's door and quietly let himself out, before closing the door to its first catch point, simply to stop it swinging open and potentially warning people that he was in the area.

By now, the sun had disappeared over the westerly horizon and he slowly moved along the sandy track leading to the ruins of the church in the manner that he had been taught to silently move on his Army Infantry course.

After another ten minutes he could clearly see the outlines of the ruins of the church, which stood out against the backdrop of the darkening blue sky of the evening. Straining every muscle in his legs, he slowly moved forward, placing each foot silently on the sandy soil before he gradually transferred his weight on to that foot.

When he was approximately twenty-five metres from the ruins of the church and just about to take pace forward, the silhouette of a man rose up in front of him. Peter froze to the spot as the silhouette of the man slowly turned and looked around, until he realized that the man was now looking straight in his direction.

Then in a voice he instantly recognized, Michael said, "I can see you, Peter. Can you see me?"

Peter straightened up from the crouched posture he had been using as he approached the ruins and answered, "Yes Michael. I can see you."

As Peter said this he heard the sound of someone struggling to move to Peter's right and a muffled voice clearly tried to say something, but the words were indistinguishable. Michael continued by saying, "And can you see who is here by my side?"

Peter answered by calling out Elena's name, which resulted in the sound of more struggling and frantic pleas through whatever was gagging her.

Knowing that Michael knew exactly where he was, Peter brought his torch up to chest height and shone it towards where he thought the struggling noises were coming from and the beam of the torch quickly found Elena, lying on top of a one metre pile of something, that Peter assumed was wood or some other inflammable substance. Elena was secured by many loops of plastic rope on top of the pile and when she knew that Peter could see her, she began to writhe aggressively, squealing as loud as she could through a cloth gag which was wrapped around her head several times.

As Peter was watching his wife struggle in her bonds, he noticed that Michael was raising both his arms and Peter clearly saw that he had an automatic pistol in his right hand and in his left he held his American Zippo cigarette lighter.

Peter stared at his nemesis as he off-handily turned the automatic pistol in his wrist and said, "This is one of my little souvenirs from our Israeli friends, who by the way, were members of the Israeli intelligence service, the Mossad, who were investigating my little side line of importing drugs into Cyprus for onward shipment to Greece and other European countries. I'm afraid you helped me kill four dedicated Mossad agents, simply because one of them had a problem with my nationality."

As Michael talked, Peter had been weighing up his options. He had noticed that every time Elena struggled to loosen the ropes which were restraining her, Michael would move his eyes towards her to see if she was having any success. Peter had decided that every time Michael's eyes were not focused on him, he would move a little bit nearer to Michael and Elena. To disguise these actions he kept the beam of his torch aimed directly into Michael's eyes and had already moved at least another five metres nearer to his target.

Michael then held up his other hand, in which he was holding his Zippo lighter and said, "It is true that I was brought up a Maronite Christian, but my father and I converted to the true faith of the Qur'an, blessed be the words of his messenger Muhammed, and we used the money we made from the drugs to help fund the activities of Hezbollah in our struggle against the Israeli and other invaders. But thanks to our dive and the discovery of the ring, I have now realized that there is a better God, who is the natural God for we Lebanese to worship and that is the great God Baal, First and Principal King of Hell. You can now watch me as I make the first sacrifice to Baal on this site for thousands of years. Since I have started to wear this ring," said Michael, holding up his left hand so that Peter could clearly see the huge ring on his middle finger, "I know that I have become the high priest to Baal and for all my actions I will be rewarded by him with a seat at the high table of the God, when I die."

As Peter watched in horror as Michael flipped open the cover of his Zippo lighter and raised his thumb to roll down the steel wheel that rubs against the flint to ignite the Zippo. Then, in an attempt to distract Michael, Peter asked, "So was it you that killed Maroulla?"

Michael looked back at him and a wry smile came to his lips. "Yes, I wanted to stop you diving in the Cape Greco area, so that you wouldn't find any more of my drug packages and I thought that if you had a funeral to arrange and attend, you would not be diving, but that was a mistake on my part, for it would never have dawned on me that a devoted son-in-law, would go straight back to diving, even before the inquest into her death was completed. I will not be so careless again. In any case, I did not like the way she run the family business. In the blessed Qur'an the wife's place is behind her man and not running his business. Oh, it was also me that ended the life of your pathetic dog. It really was not fitting for an ex-soldier like you to have such a weak dog. You should have had a hunting dog, which befits a valiant soldier such as you."

In the few minutes that Michael had been talking, and been distracted by Elena's struggles and plaintive cries through her gag, Peter had managed to move closer to his quarry and by this time was only about ten metres away from him.

At this point, Michael again held up the Zippo lighter in his left hand and once more prepared to light it with his thumb on the wheel.

Peter desperately tried to think of something that would once again distract Michael from his evil intentions, but with no pause in his mental plans, he decided it would soon be time for action, so he tensed himself to make the twenty-five metre charge in an attempt to grasp the lighter and stop Michael setting fire to the sacrificial offering.

Suddenly Michael twisted his left hand around so that the Zippo lighter again became the focus of all of Peter's attention. As Michael waved the Zippo above his head in an obvious threat that he would soon light the fire, both men began to hear a distant rumbling sound that although indistinct had a deep base note and was also causing a slight vibration through the soil they were standing on.

Michael's face turned into a vicious sneer as he cried out, "Now is the moment for the sacrifice. Say goodbye to your lovely Elena."

As the rumbling sound grew louder and louder, Michael spun the wheel of the Zippo lighter, which ignited the petrol of the wick of the lighter and a bright flame grew up from the ignite fuel. He turned and with a toss of his left hand threw the lighter at the base of the sacrificial pyre. He must have previously used some form of fire accelerant on the wood, for the wood instantly caught fire and the flames began to move higher in the stack of wood.

Peter immediately threw the torch he had been holding into the face of Michael, who had begun to back away from the fire the moment caught alight. As he did so he became aware that the rumbling sound, which was coming from the direction of the sea was getting louder and louder.

Michael threw his left arm up to deflect the torch which was heading accurately towards his face, then he turned to face Peter and raised the pistol towards him. Suddenly, from the corner of his eye, Peter noticed that Elena had somehow managed to free herself from some of the ropes that bound her and she pulled down the thick cloth gag from her mouth. As the sound of the rumbling was by this time very distinct and also had a higher pitched whistling component, Elena sat up in the growing flames of the fire and in a voice that sounded totally alien to her, but a language that Peter quickly realized was ancient Greek, she said loudly and clearly, "I am the Goddess Aphrodite, the beloved daughter of my father Zeus. I rule the over the love of men and the waves of the sea and will not allow my people to suffer at the hands of an unrighteous God."

At that moment the deafening rumbling sound was transformed into an enormous tsunami of sea water, which burst against the cliffs below the ruins of the church and a large wave carried over the cliffs and hit the fire with great force.

Peter was the first to react to this turn of events and he grabbed hold of Michael's right hand, which held the pistol and pushed it away from his body, while at the same time he landed a very heavy punch directly on to Michael's nose. As he was drawing his fist back to land another punch, Peter realized that the first blow had already broken Michael's nose, for there was already a large amount of blood pouring down over his mouth.

Michael ceased struggling to get the pistol back under his control and with a loud cry of pain moved his left hand to protect his nose from further damage, which allowed Peter to hit him with an enormous punch to the stomach, followed quickly by a kick between the legs, which was delivered with all the pent up rage that he had inside him.

Michael by this time was clearly losing the fight and seemed to have completely forgotten that he had a pistol in his right hand. Knowing that he now had complete control of the fight, Peter continued to wreak his vengeance on his smaller opponent. He kicked the thigh of one leg so hard that Michael immediately lost control of his leg and fell to the ground. At that moment, Peter was able to spare the time to look towards Elena and when he was sure that she was in no kind of danger, he continued to punch and kick Michael into total submission. After landing another heavy blow to the nose, Peter managed to grab Michael's right arm with both hands and with all the strength he could muster he slammed the arm down onto his knew and felt the bones of the lower arm snap from the injury. The pistol fell from Michael's hand and the threat Michael posed to Peter and Elena fell away with it.

Knowing that he was now in total control of the fight, Peter grabbed Michael's left hand and with a very quick manoeuvre, managed to pull the ring free from Michael's finger, to which Michael voiced a pitiful scream of protest, as Peter turned towards the sea and threw the ring as hard as he could over the cliff.

Michael somehow managed to raise himself on to his feet and with a cry of rage ran as fast as he could to the edge of the cliff, in a final rash gesture of defiance and as he reached the edge of the cliff, he briefly stopped and looked down into the darkness below him before he threw himself off the cliff in an attempt to catch the falling ring.

A moment later, there was the sickening sound of Michael's body being smashed on to the sharp rocks directly infront of Chapel Cave.

Epilogue
Monday, 7th August 2017

The television programme started with an attractive young lady announcer saying that she would be reading the local Cyprus news for Monday the seventh of August 2017. She first read out several items of local news, which started with a report on a visit to Limassol by the President of Cyprus, Mr. Nicos Anastasiades, who had opened a new ward to the city's hospital. It showed Mr. Anastasiades cutting the ribbon to open the ward and his wife being given a huge bouquet of flowers to mark the event. The local news continued with other items of interest to the general population of Cyprus, before the young lady announced that the next item would be in the series of reports about obscure but popular tourist destinations by their local Ayia Napa correspondent, Costas Stephanidies. The image on the screen quickly changed to a good looking young man, with his back to the entrance to the newly restored and reconsecrated church of Ayioi Anargiroi. Costas was holding up, just above his waist a microphone, covered in a thick felt sock.

He smiled at the camera infront of him and started his report by saying, "Hello everyone. I am Costas Stephanidies reporting from the newly restored church of

Ayioi Anargiroi, which is just north of the tip of Cape Greco on the south-easterly tip of Cyprus.

This beautiful church was destroyed by fire in the summer of 1987 and it has taken this long to fully restore it to the splendour of its original build."

The reporter continued by slowly walking to the open blue door of the church, where a local priest was standing.

Turning to face the camera, the reporter continued, "This is Father Demitrios, who is responsible for the church."

At that moment, the reporter turned to face the old bearded Greek priest and the cameraman moved the television camera so that the viewers could see both the reporter and the priest. The reporter moved the microphone so that it could pick up the comments of both men and said, "Father Demitrios, can you please tell us of what has happened to this wonderful church since it was destroyed by fire in 1987."

The old priest looked into the lens of the camera and told of how the church was mysteriously destroyed by fire and although there had been a long investigation by the police, they could find no evidence of arson and so the case remains open in their books. Initially, it took some years for the Archbishop of Cyprus to find the money to restore the church to its former glory. Eventually, the rebuilding of the church started in 1998, then when the building was sound and the roof was in place, the magnificent wooden fixtures were added, having been skilfully made by local carpenters in Paralimni. In the meantime, replacement icons were commissioned from the monks in various Cyprus monasteries, including Kyko monastery and Stavrovouni monastery. One icon was even made in Russia, in the little village of Palekh, which is in Siberia. These icons, with their silver and semi-precious adornments, were the hardest items to recreate, to ensure that they were identical replicas of the icons that had originally adorned the church. But now the church was once again complete and faithfully restored to its original splendour and was officially rededicated by the current Archbishop of Cyprus, Archbishop Chrysostomos II, in the year 2016."

As the old priest paused to draw a deep breath before continuing his history of the rebuild of the church, the reporter politely pulled the microphone away from him and without causing too much embarrassment he continued by saying, "Thank you very much Father Demitrios for all the facts you have given us about the restoration of the church. I have heard on good authority that the church is now a very popular site for tourists to visit when they come to our beautiful island. What exactly brings them to this remote church built on a rocky headland so near to the sea?"

Father Demitrios smiled as he reached out and took control of the microphone again before saying, "I often ask our visitors that question and invariably I am told that they have been advised by tour guides that the view of the church, with the blue Mediterranean Sea behind it, is what really draws them to visit the church." After a short pause he added, "The other thing they often mention is that they come to see the hermit who lives in the cave below the church."

This appeared to raise the interest of the reporter, exactly as he had been rehearsed by the director and he asked the priest to tell him about the hermit who lived in the cave.

Father Demitrios looked once more into the lens of the television camera and said, "Father Petros is the old hermit who has chosen to live in the cave below the church. He has been living there since 1987, but, unfortunately, the years have not been kind to him, especially as he has been living and sleeping in the cave for all those thirty years."

Without waiting for the priest to add any more details, the reporter pulled back the microphone and the cameraman shifted the focus of the camera back on to a narrow framed shot of the reporter, who continued by saying, "Well, let us now move along this newly laid paved walkway, which will lead us down into the cave below the church."

As he spoke he took a few paces backwards along the newly-laid paved path, which had hand rails on both sides, and turned to face down the path towards the cave. The cameraman followed him down the path swinging the camera to both sides in order to show the viewers the impressive view from the clifftop, as the reporter spoke a few platitudes of political correctness by stating that although the path had been beautifully laid in compliance with guidance from Public Health advisors, the path was really not suitable to wheelchair users, unless their carers were able to carry them over the steeper sections of the climb, down into the cave.

As the reporter reached the point where the path turned right around a steep sharp bend, he paused with his back to the railing and said, "Just below me are the rocks where shortly after the church burned down in 1987, a young Lebanese tourist fell to his death on the sharp rocks below."

As he continued along the path, down into the cave and while turning around to face the camera, his feet slipped down the smooth rock of the floor of the cave, which resulted in the reporter involuntarily making a little cry of fear. The reporter quickly recovered control of himself and speaking into the microphone once more said, "As you can see, the floor of the cave is very slippery, due to the wear it has suffered over the countless years from hermits and tourists, which has resulted in the smoothing down of the rock with their feet."

The cameraman then panned around the cave, as the reporter continued, "Unfortunately Father Petros is not in the cave this afternoon, as he was found unconscious, lying on the rocky floor by a tourist a few days ago and is now in Paralimni hospital being treated for exposure and various other complaints, linked to his living in this barren cave. But I have been talking to various people who know him well and they have told me that he has indeed been living in the cave since 1987. No one really know why he has chosen to live the life of a hermit in this cave for all these years, but I have heard that he sits all day, simply staring out to sea and only seems to break away from his concentration on the sea, when people jump off the cliffs into the bay infront of the cave, or when scuba divers enter or leave the water from the cave. At those moments, he becomes very agitated and shouts at the divers, saying, they must not bring any old artefacts they find, out of the sea. In some cases, he even insists on frisking people for ancient treasures, before he will let them leave the cave. He has been doing this for many years, living alone in this hostile environment, supported only by his aged wife, who is called Elena."

Printed in Germany
by Amazon Distribution
GmbH, Leipzig